Tales from Glory's Hole

By Drace Domino

Written By Drace Domino

twitter.com/Drace_Domino

Cover and Illustrations By Cholie

twitter.com/CholieNSFW

Edited By Charlie Knight

cknightwrites.com

Special thanks to Gee…and to Ryah!

Both of whom are awesome.

Content Warning:

Light Fantasy Violence

Sexual Situations

For everyone whose

favorite shipping trope is

monster/person that fucks monsters.

That's the good stuff.

Half Snake, All Heart

From wall to wall, the quaint little tavern in the dead center of Clover is packed with guests. A cluster of elves sit playing a board game with marble and glass pieces, a mingled group of dwarves and humans engage in a drinking contest near the back, and a trio of Daru women whisper among themselves while they gaze across the crowd, no doubt trying to decide which patrons they'll take as a lover tonight.

It's a tavern of crowded delights, of mirth and joy that only a combination of genuine warmth and cheap ale can foster. Smiling faces. Bellowing laughs. And of course, fond exchanges between future paramours. In truth, it's a little overwhelming; Clover's quite the big city and fairly diverse to boot, and there you sit in the most crowded bar surrounded by the noise of strangers. Curious but alone.

As a mug slides across the table with a foamy head, filled with a beer that carries the sweet smell of honey, you're offered a brief reminder. At Glory's Hole, nobody is truly alone, not while the dwarf that keeps the doors open is there.

"Looks like a long journey's brought ya here, friend." The braided black loops of hair at the back of her head bounce as she settles into place, though the motion is put to shame by the much more noticeable swing of a plump chest barely contained within the embrace of a tight-fitting tunic. Freckled features offer a pleased smile as she nudges the drink to you once more with an insistency that suggests she'll forcibly put it in your hand before too long. "Sorry you have to see the place on a slow night like this."

You lift your brow as you gaze once more across the bar. There's already barely enough room for people to move, and the mere act of squeezing in between tables is a snug enough fit that it could start a love connection. Regardless, the dwarf woman gives a slow sigh as she leans against the bar and drums her fingers atop it. After a few short seconds of watching her bar thrive during what she considers a slow night, she finally speaks up anew, this time moving a hand to bump her knuckles against your arm.

"How about a story?" she asks, confirming yet another rumor you've heard of the establishment. The dwarf loves to talk, and she isn't particularly shy about refilling a patron's drink so long as they sit there and listen. Sure enough, right after you take a sip of the honeyed beer she poured you, she claims the mug once more, unnecessarily refreshing it from a nearby keg while gazing over her shoulder. "Look over there. Y'know what that reminds me of?"

A glance in the direction she gestures is reveals one of the Daru women making their move. She's a towering mountain of a woman as most Daru are, well-muscled and toned, and standing at seven feet of intimidating glory. She's chatting up an elf at the board game table that seems almost instantly enchanted, twirling her fingers around locks of beautiful silver-blue hair and even stretching out a hand to trace her touch across the Daru's arm.

Anyone can tell - you, the dwarf, the other Daru, and the rest of the visibly awkward-feeling elves at the board game table - the Daru will be taking that young lady home tonight. Whether it's a matter of chatty dwarves or the boundless hunger of passionate amazons, it seems like a night for proving rumors true.

When you look back at the dwarf, she's settled onto a stool behind the bar, a wistful look in her eyes as she tidily cleans out a used mug. "Nothing quite so soothing as a love story, right?" she asks with a smile, briefly flashing the metal stud nestled in the center of her tongue. "All the better if it's between some adorable slip of a thing and a real mountain of a woman like her. Well...since it's your first time here at Glory's Hole, I've got just the story to share with you."

She sets down the mug, leans back on her stool until the wooden legs creak under her sturdy physique, and smirks when she catches you stealing another glimpse at generous dwarven bust.

"Enjoy your drink. This is one of my favorites, and it's all about finding love...and how someone can slither right into your heart."

At Glory's Hole, the beer was cheap, and the stories were free - and each had a tendency to leave a sticky residue on the countertop.

How long she had been running, Alena couldn't tell. It felt like she had been rushing through the wilds for hours now, and even a body made strong by a lifetime of farm labor was starting to weaken and slow. She was wearing the scrapes and bruises that could only come from a panicked charge through the most dangerous region of Rugget outside the Bile Pools, but every time she stumbled in the heavy brush leading to the Feral Hills, she managed to crawl back up and keep running. She had to. It didn't matter how tired she grew, and it didn't matter what dangers were waiting in the ominous hillside before her. All that mattered was that she escaped her home...and that she never, ever looked back.

This day had been coming for some time now, and she still wasn't as prepared as she hoped. The heavy rucksack on her back was filled with as many preserved supplies as she could steal from her family's cupboard, though Alena knew that she was no survivalist. Her bag was probably filled with too many bundles of dried beef and not enough flint or bandages, and the further she ran, the more she thought of other items she should have brought for her flight from home. All were afterthoughts that didn't strike her mind until she was miles away, any of which could be an oversight big enough to cost the girl her life.

Did she bring enough gold? Did she bring any silver in case she encountered lycanthropes? What about antivenom? There were snakes in the Feral Hills, and she *detested* snakes. The poor girl's mind continued to spin with items forgotten or overlooked, and the weight of worry added to the impact of her footsteps. It was already hard enough to keep running with sore joints, exhausted muscles, and scraped skin...but now that she was second guessing herself, it just might have been too much for her to endure.

It wasn't until the girl reached the dense forest at the base of the Feral Hills that she finally stopped, pausing long enough to lean her head and arms against a massive tree so she could struggle to catch her breath. No doubt back home, the search parties had already begun, and though she had purposefully waded through rivers to throw off the scent, her family's hounds were famous for their tracking. They'd find her sooner or later if she didn't keep up her distance.

The run ahead would be even harder than the run behind, but it was one she needed to make. If she could only skirt the edges of the Feral Hills long enough to get to the elven city of Glint, then she could rest. A rest she was already craving more than any that came before in nearly two decades of life.

"Hahh...hahh…" Alena panted, slowly sliding down to her knees at the base of that mighty tree. The weight of her rucksack worked to pull her down, and she shrugged it gently from her shoulders to dismiss the bulk of it for the moment. Every part of her hurt - from the worn muscles to the burning lungs to her sore feet to the stinging at the corners of her eyes. For hours, she had been pushing through heartache and strain just so she could reach the boundary of the Feral Hills knowing full-well it was a place so dangerous and wild that no right-minded person would ever set foot within.

And yet...returning home would be worse.

"Hnng...oof!" The girl made a gentle noise as she twisted and flopped down, letting her rump land against the ground below as she wedged her back to the tree. The forest's edge gave her a reasonable enough vantage point to watch the fields she'd fled through - even if she realized that she could add a spyglass to the list of things she forgot to pack. With weary arms, the girl pulled her rucksack up and opened it to rummage for food and drink, still with her chest racing as she recovered from the long, hard run.

"Al...almost...almost there. Hard part's over, Alena."

She was lying to herself. If anything? The hard part was only beginning, and the harsh wilds of the Feral Hills were already buzzing with the knowledge that a human had entered the region.

She wouldn't be the first runaway from the Homestead to meet a grisly end amongst the hills. She would simply be the next if the beasts already drawing in her scent had any say in the matter.

Alena didn't make it a single evening before she was running again, this time with far more urgency than before. It didn't matter now what items she forgot to bring, for her rucksack was still laying at the base of that mighty tree, completely abandoned in the hopes of survival. Now, in the near-pitch black of night in the woods at the base of the Feral Hills, Alena stumbled and whimpered as she pushed forward with every ounce of the strength remaining within her. That morning, she was running for her freedom. Now, she was running for her life.

"Hawwwwoooooo!" The howls of the gnolls were behind her, filled with a hunger that she had no intention of sating. As the girl ran, she was forced to keep wiping the tears from her eyes, and even in that newfound urgency, the weight of her emotions were pushing down on her. If only she had stayed at home and did as her parents wanted. If only she did what was best for her family. Wasn't a miserable, boring life better than getting eaten by gnolls in the wild?!

For now, she was in too much of a panic to suss out the answer, but that didn't stop those dangerous thoughts from making her stumble every other step. Each time she heard the branches behind her snap or the heavy sound of paws thudding against the ground, Alena pushed herself forward with renewed fear and panic. And every time one of the gnolls's howls filled the air, her entire body tensed in horror that chilled her to a primal core.

"Hawwwwwooooooo!"

"No, no, no, go away!" Alena screamed.

Just a few steps ahead, she saw a felled tree in her path. It took every last bit of her strength, but she managed to slap her hands against it and vault over, falling hard on the other side with a loud, sharp squeak. Pain rioted through her as she landed on her ankle and it twisted from the impact, sending her cascading into the wet leaves and fallen branches. Her red pigtail braids danced, and her glasses went spinning from her face as she fell, that fit farmgirl body cast hard to the ground. Unfortunately, the sound of her cries only drew the attention of all the gnolls pursuing her, and when she lifted her head, she saw what was most likely the last thing all runaways saw in the woods of the Feral Hills. Or at least, the muddied image of their final sight as offered through squinting, tear-filled eyes.

In the dark of night and without her glasses, ominous shadows ruled her vision. She could see the massive figure of the felled tree that marked the end of her escape, and then, moving in slow, predatory fashion, a series of gaunt, hunched figures prowling in a circle around her. Their forms were difficult to make out, but the gleam in their eyes certainly wasn't, and as Alena looked around, she counted six, seven, eight of the beasts focusing on her. When she scrambled to get up, her twisted ankle immediately betrayed her, and once more she was sent to the ground with a heavy thud - this time, to the twisted, feral laughing of the jackal-like abominations circling her.

"Heeewwwwhehehe!" their shoulders rose and fell with cruel bliss, and as a collective pack, they inched all the closer. Alena could smell the revolting stench of wet fur, study their sinister, burning eyes, nearly feel their breath upon her, and as she looked from one end of the line to the other, she knew what a hopeless situation she had found herself in. Even as she tried to press her back against the tree, two more of the beasts hopped up on it from behind, making the weight of it press all the harder against the ground below.

"N-No, no...no, please...I just…" Effectively blinded without her glasses and downed by her twisted ankle, Alena had turned herself into truly helpless prey. The gnolls didn't even have to scratch her to show just how deadly the Feral Hills could be and just how out of place a farmer from the Homestead was there. If only she had chosen to run to Clover instead. She wouldn't have made it far in the city before her father's hounds tracked her, but...but at least she'd be alive long enough to be forced back home. Now? Now, Alena could only hope that these beasts would end her suffering quickly. "Please...please let me go… I'll run, I'll never come back, I...I...n-n-no, please, I…"

Her pleas fell on deaf ears, if the gnolls even understood her to begin with. As she scrambled for safety, the beasts suddenly charged forward, lunging after her with fury in their voice and a fierce weight to their charging pounce. One after the other, the gnolls dove towards her, landing against the ground beside that massive, felled tree. She could feel revolting, claw-adorned hands wrap around her wrists and ankles while others shoved her shoulders down. They were going to flay and devour her right then and there, and none of it was going to matter anymore. Not her stubborn refusal to step in line with her siblings, not her rejection of the family farm, not her constant fighting with her father and mother, not...not anything.

What she wouldn't give for the worries of a simple farmgirl in that moment.

Alena was sure that her end was near as she felt the gnolls' breath against her throat, and she looked up through the haze to see the gleam of their wicked fangs. But just before they sunk their teeth against her flesh to begin their grim and shrieking feast, there was a sudden rumble from underneath them all. The ground shook and, before any of them were able to discern exactly what happened, started to collapse.

Weakened by the weight of the tree and the sudden pouncing of the pack of gnolls, the unstable soil started to fall from underneath them. She could hear their yelps and feel their claws scrape against her while they desperately tried to keep their footing, but before long, both hunter and prey were of the same status: plummeting down, riding a landslide into a deep, dark cave. For once, the screams of the gnolls were joining in with Alena's own, playing melody with the sound of that fallen tree crashing through the dirt and beginning a violent slide. Lost in a blizzard of wet leaves, left dizzy by the flurry of activity in the darkness, and still reeling with pain, Alena wasn't able to track everything that happened. She only knew she was falling...and she knew she was screaming.

And she knew that in the split-second before she hit the ground, far, far below, she could see light. A dull, strange, warm purple...and then darkness once more as she landed with a brutal thud.

With a pounding head, Alena was woken by the sounds of struggle. As she fought with every ounce of strength within her to open her eyes, the poor thing was left trying to put together the pieces of what just happened. She remembered the cries of those horrible gnolls, she remembered the ground crumbling underneath their feet, and she remembered purple light. Soft, gentle, and almost comforting as she tumbled.

And now, with her eyes finally opening, she saw that the light was still there...and it was exposing a scene straight from her nightmares.

"Harrrooowww!" The gnolls were there with her in the strange, subterranean cave that they had all fallen into. Surrounding them on all sides were mushrooms of various sizes - some as tiny as the ones that grew back on the farm, and some that towered as high as her father's old silo. Each one of them was some variant of red or blue or purple, and without deviation, they all carried a dull glow which worked to bathe the area in a subtle light. Considering what Alena was seeing, she almost wished they didn't.

With her glasses lost, Alena couldn't exactly make out the monstrous scene before her, but she could see enough to feel overtaken by fear. The furry, lithe figures of the gnolls were engaged in battle against something massive - something with a long, serpentine tail that could only be the thing of nightmares. She saw a gargantuan coil of snakeflesh weaving across the cave floor, shimmering with scales of crimson and indigo, beautiful save for the terror they conveyed. While the gnolls threw themselves against it, the tail made swift work of flicking them away with hundreds of pounds of muscle, easily launching them to the sides of the cave with deafening cracking noises or simply throwing them high up into the air. They landed with sickening crashes to the stone below.

Panic filled Alena once more, and with a sinking feeling in the pit of her stomach, the girl tried to lay as low as possible. In truth, she knew she should have run. She should have picked a random direction and charged ahead, exploiting the fact that the gnolls were distracted by this titanic beast filling the cave. She was so frozen with fear, however, that all she could do was dig her fingers deep into the bed of moss she'd landed on and watch the blurry scene unfold with her mouth agape and her heart racing.

Screams. Howls. The gnashing of teeth and the breaking of bones. Somehow, it was the yelps of pain that were the worst as this titanic creature dismissed the gnolls with astonishing brutality and ease. It was treating these feral stalkers of flesh like nothing more than trivial insects, and Alena still had yet to see anything more than that powerful, whiplike tail. She could only imagine just what the rest of this monster looked like.

When there was only a single gnoll remaining, the wiry creature set its gaze upon Alena and made a desperate charge in her direction. It was impossible for the girl to decipher the madness of its decision. Perhaps it intended to throw her to the snake in order to buy itself some time, perhaps it simply wanted to see the human dead before its own last second came. Maybe it wanted just one last meal in the form of a hastily-bitten and gulped chunk of farmgirl flesh. Regardless, it didn't get what it was after.

Just as the creature drew near enough to pounce on the red headed human, that massive tail lurking in the dull glow of the cave lurched forward once more. With incredible might, it moved to coil around the gnoll, spinning its impressive frame around that lithe form once, twice, three times until...snap! There was a tiny cracking noise that came from the creature, muffled by the hundreds of pounds of snake flesh that encircled it.

With tears in her eyes, Alena watched the final gnoll drop to the floor and that mighty tail once more retreat to the shadows of the cave. With no other prey among the mushrooms, Alena could only assume that she would be the next to go, the final target of a horrific, monstrous beast lurking underneath the Feral Hills. The sole benefactor of her desperate rush through the woods, all thanks to a particularly tall cavern with a loose, unstable ceiling. Though her chance of escape was minimal with her sprained ankle and her lost glasses, she still fumbled against the ground, trying to force herself to her feet as she strained to look from side to side.

Mushrooms...moss...mushrooms...moss.

"No, no...there's...there's got to be a way out, I…" Squinting, the girl lifted her head and peered up, hoping to see the light of the stars and moon - enough to suggest that she wasn't all that far away from the surface. Unfortunately, she was greeted only with the same cold darkness. Unforgiving. Terrifying. Merciless. "I can't...can't do this, I…"

Alena leaned heavily on one of the larger mushrooms, taking care not to put any weight on her sprained ankle. At the same moment that her fingers sunk against its spongy side, a slithering noise came from just beyond it, and it sent her into such a fright that she stumbled right back down, launching herself onto her backside on the mossy rock below. Fear was overtaking her. The scream that filled the cavern was no doubt a foolish idea considering the monster was still lurking nearby, and yet she couldn't stop herself from letting it pass her lips. As she collapsed to the ground, the girl gazed forward with widening eyes. Something was emerging from behind the mushroom, and she didn't need her glasses to see it.

"M'lsss etop? Husss bintala."

The figure that emerged from hiding wasn't the grotesque, towering snake head that Alena had suspected, but a woman. She was tall with pale skin and shrouded in a long-sleeved white robe tied loosely around a curvy waist and the hood pulled high upon her head. A pair of brown braids hung down the sides of her head not too unlike Alena's own, although while the farmgirl's reached the small of her back, this new woman's only dropped to just below her chin. Her eyes were kind, her cheeks were chubby, and her lips the shade of a fresh peach - so striking and gentle that, for the moment, Alena didn't notice the rest of her. The beautiful woman drew closer and stretched a hand outward, offering something to the smaller girl as she spoke anew.

"Bintala. Bintala tisss."

Alena didn't understand a word, though when she looked to the woman's open hand, she saw something that made her tremendously happy. Resting in her outstretched palm with little more than a light scratch on a single lens were the round, wide-lensed glasses she had lost in the struggle. Alena didn't hesitate to snatch them back, her eyes shining as she pulled them up to slip them right back onto her face.

"My glasses! Oh, thank you so much, miss!" Still riding the adrenaline of the moment, there were glaring things she didn't notice until just about that very second. "But...but we need to run! There's something in here, and it--ahhhhh!"

Alena's glasses nearly fell right back off her face as she launched herself backwards yet again, pushing against the nearest mushroom. In the dim light afforded in the cave and with her sight newly restored, Alena could take in the full form of her kind benefactor - from the sweet, chubby features of the robed woman to where her body flowed into that of a massive snake, starting at about her waist. Crimson and purple scales shimmered in the ambient light of the mushrooms, but there was no time for Alena to appreciate the beauty of it.

The woman before her was half-serpent, and such a horror had never even been whispered about by the people of the Homestead. For as much as farmer parents relied on scary stories to prevent their children from wandering off too far, for all the tales of ghosts in the Endless Nightmare Frst and the oozes of the Bile Pools and those lawless pirates at Port Failure, *this* was a monster altogether new.

Monstrous or not, the snake-woman didn't seem to be offended by Alena's fear. While the human girl panicked and cowered against the mushroom, the mighty creature slithered from behind the line of mushrooms, allowing every inch of her to fall into the girl's sight. With frightening dexterity and speed, she coiled the majority of her length underneath herself, sitting upright like a cobra waiting to strike even though she seemed far from doing anything of the sort. Instead, she simply folded her hands at her front and gave the girl a little bow, speaking again in a strange dialect with a pronounced lisp to her voice.

"M'lsss vogun," she offered, and tilted her head while studying the other woman. "Gar...gar gosssenna?"

Alena, who was quite surprised to find that she wasn't already being messily devoured, finally started to calm down. Her breathing slowed to a manageable rate, and she let her muscles ease, looking at the strange, mysterious creature that now rested on her coils before her. This...this woman meant her no harm. Alena was smart enough to tell as much once she finally calmed down.

Shifting in her position, Alena turned her head to mirror the serpent's gaze, and she offered the kindest smile possible for a girl that had been through the sort of day she had suffered through. "Hi," she finally offered, and gave her new friend a single, tiny nod. "Thank you."

She was already changing her opinion about snakes.

***

Alena had hoped her farming days were behind her, and yet...this? This, she didn't mind so much. Nearly two weeks to the day from her fall through the surface and into the mushroom cave, the young woman's hands sunk deep into a patch of soil, mixing a few shards of red mushroom meat within. There was a heavily spicy aroma to the air not uncommon to the peppers they used to grow a few farms away from her father's, just enough for her to remember what things were like back then and then to quickly realize just how good she had it now.

She was still underground, so deep and dark within the tunnels below the Feral Hills that it was unlikely she'd see the sun again even if she ever wanted to - a prospect that was increasingly more unlikely with every passing day. The Underhills had everything she could possibly want between an endless supply of delicious mushrooms, plenty of fresh water for drinking and fishing via underground springs and rivers, and a constant, cool temperature that kept her perfectly comfortable. As the girl knelt there with her long red braids dangling over her shoulders and her glasses perched atop her nose, she even hummed sweetly while she worked, continuing to till the soil with a smile.

The home she had known for the past two weeks was tiny but cozy. A small grotto deep within the underhill with a freshwater river just a dozen feet away and a smooth, flat stone that she had padded with salvaged supplies and a thick bed of moss. She had even spent the time decorating it by planting some of the prettiest mushrooms she could find - an array of gold and purple lights that ebbed and flowed with radiance as the hours passed, serving as her surrogate morning and night. It was quaint. It was simple. And it was home.

And home would be nothing without someone to share it with.

"M'lsss~" The familiar voice of the serpent woman rose from behind Alena, though she didn't flinch when she heard it. Her smile only intensified while she dipped her hand into the bucket of shredded spicy mushrooms, scooping a few more to continue tilling the soil. She didn't tremble or cower even when she heard that enormous snake form glide behind her, nor did she look over her shoulder as the powerful creature blocked the glow of the mushrooms while she loomed high above. Instead, Alena kept working, pretending not to hear with a coy smile on her lips as that soothing, kind, lisping voice escaped again. “M’lsss Alena. Tovusss garto.”

The human, with her hands deep in the soil, continued to play ignorant while that mighty, purple-scaled tail coiled around the tiny garden and the girl tending to it. The elegant and surprisingly graceful form of the serpent swept around her with a wide circle, drawing closer and closer like the walls of a tower collapsing in on her. Still, Alena continued to hum and till up to the point that the serpent pulled herself before her, popping her face just before the redhead’s so she could not be ignored.

“Tovus garto...I see you, I see you~” Alena finally broke her jest, giggling when that hooded face dropped before her once more. Every bit as pretty as she was the day they met, with chocolate braids hanging to her cheeks and kindly, chubby features sported on her face, the serpent beamed. Alena’s smile was similarly undeniable as she beheld her friend, and when the serpent stretched a hand forward, she didn’t recoil, instead moving to press her cheek against the warm, outstretched palm. A pleasant sigh escaped the back of her throat.

“How did it go, Pechessa?”

“Tot! Lisss nevra, Alena.” The serpent continued to cradle her friend’s cheek in her palm, holding it there for a long, appreciative moment before casting a heavy rucksack from her shoulder. As she tossed it aside, Alena could easily peek within, seeing that it was filled with everything on the scavenging shopping list. A bundle of fish from the traps they set three caves down, some of those particularly delicious orange-capped mushrooms that tasted of fresh citrus, and more rope from the flotsam that washed up on at the distant edge of the tunnels.

The serpent Pechessa beamed proudly at her haul but wasn't quite done showing it off. Her free hand dipped down and into the baggy pocket of her white robe, and when it came free anew, she revealed out a brilliant blue flower with crystal-patterned fronds clipped high on the stem for the purposes of moving it upward and nestling it at the edge of Alena's ear.

The human girl just watched with a rapidly-intensifying blush as the serpent affixed the flower to her hair, nibbling on her bottom lip while the space between them closed. Her hands lifted from the soil and swiftly wiped themselves off at the edge of her work apron, and once they were clean, she braced them to the sides of the titanic snake body that surrounded her on all sides. With blue in her hair and red on her cheeks, Alena could only stare ahead at Pechessa with a quiver in her throat that she was still sussing out.

"Thank you," she whispered, and her fingers teased down the smooth, strong scales of the other woman's body. Soon, her eyes closed, and her head dipped forward, only to be met in a gentle embrace by that of the other. Human and serpent nuzzled their foreheads while Alena whispered, nervous and charmed in equal measure, "You...you're always so kind to me."

"M'lsss," the whisper returned from the other just as her fingers passed down Alena's cheek once more. The coil of her magnificent figure shifted and loosened, and Pechessa dipped her head inward, as if trying to hide bashfully underneath the edge of her hood. She uncoiled herself entirely from the loose circle she had formed around Alena and let her enormous tail stretch lazily across the stone of the cave floor, her upper half positioning itself just beside the girl. She gazed down at the recently tilled soil and pointed a hand to the mix, speaking in a language that the human still didn't know. Not that it mattered much; thus far, communicating between the two had been a joyful way for two new friends to share their hours. "Kala tizza? Chora den."

"Mhm," Alena cooed and nodded, even without knowing the words. She gestured to the half-emptied bucket of shredded spicy mushroom and dusted her hands off anew. Once she had, she couldn't stop herself from lifting one palm up to keep fidgeting with the flower positioned in her hair, stroking her fingers over the petals and toying daintily with it while she spoke. "Back on the farm, we mixed peppers in with the soil surrounding our fields. It kept the gophers away because they hated the smell, and I'm *betting* that it'll be the same deal with those little monsters that have been stealing your beets."

It seemed like even if Pechessa didn't share her language, the serpent woman understood well enough. She offered a bright and beaming smile from underneath the hood upon the realization that their pest problems were stymied and soon began to creep down to what had become the shared living quarters of the pair. Mostly flat rocks with comfortable accessories with Pechessa herself able to drape just about anywhere she liked. As Alena walked to join her, she couldn't help but move with a small spring in her step. In her old life snakes always unnerved her, but now? She was getting increasingly comfortable with the sound of slithering on any one side of her.

"M'lsss?" Pechessa's voice spoke up as she settled down, coiling into a 'sitting' position and folding her hands within her lap. She bent in such a way that a part of her tail was at the perfect height for Alena to sit on - which the human moved to do, delighted. As the pigtailed redhead hopped up onto the powerful, purple scale-covered muscle, Pechessa spoke again, one hand stretching forward in fluid fashion to give a little poke at the human's belly. "Gekko sssa?"

"No, no, I'm not hungry," came the sweet reply, and Alena shook her head while she rubbed her belly. "Breakfast was delicious. It always is."

What came next between the two women was something that Alena had come to expect - and something that she looked forward to immensely. For nearly every day of the past two weeks, the two new friends spent quiet time together, simply talking, trying to teach each other words in their respective languages or simply...looking at each other. Admiring how different they were. Wondering just what could have brought them into this unique friendship that they were both so very, very comfortable in.

Some days, Pechessa spoke at length about topics that would likely forever remain a mystery to the human. Others, Alena would go on and on about life on the farm. Her parents and her siblings, her complete disdain for farming life, the way the wealthy of Clover treated the people of the Homestead like servants. It didn't matter what she rambled about; Pechessa seemed every bit as enchanted by Alena's rustic dialect as Alena was with the way her serpentine friend drug out her s sounds. Back home, Alena would've been forced to have endless conversations with people she could fully understand and intensely loathed. But this? Deep underground, alone and secluded, sitting with the most unusual creature she had ever met...this was where she was meant to be.

Two weeks in, and Alena already knew that she wasn't ever going back. She sat, she listened to Pechessa's stories, and she toyed with the flower set against her hair - a momento from someone she was growing to adore.

***

Two weeks became two months, and still, Alena was merry in the glow of the underground mushrooms. That afternoon, one of their favorite tunnels was filled with the sound of her laughter, not to mention the heavy footsteps of an eager human running at full speed. She was leading the way with Pechessa's hand firmly in her own, and even though the serpent could've easily outpaced her, she didn't seem to mind Alena setting the path ahead. Her own voice filled the tunnel from time to time as well but in a softer tone with a shy demeanor as she always seemed to tend towards.

That particular tunnel was special. Filled with some of the largest mushrooms in the entire underhill, a few of those resilient caps pushed all the way up to the roof of the tunnel. With the strength of an oak and a lifespan counted in centuries, several of those mushrooms had put enough pressure on the ceiling above that cracks had started to form. Not direct enough to let in the light or weaken the ceiling like the cave they first met in, but on the days after heavy rainfalls, it wasn't uncommon to see a makeshift waterfall dancing down the slopes of the mushroom caps as some river far above them flooded. It was never enough to cause problems in their tiny underground paradise, but always gave the pair a taste of the fresh surface world above. It was about all that Alena could tolerate, and only so long as she had her dearest friend in tow.

Sure enough, that afternoon things were no different. The tunnel floor was damp and slippery, and near the back of the cave, the largest mushrooms had lines of water dancing from the edges of the caps in a beautiful display of natural glory. The subtle glow they offered was enhanced all the more by the freshwater framing their radiance, making a post-rainfall glimpse of this particular cave among the most romantic Alena had ever seen. So distracted she was that in the midst of her run, one of her boots pressed too hard on an unstable rock, and the girl gave a yelp as she suddenly tumbled toward the stone below.

She never hit the floor. Alena had only barely started to fall before a purple tail swept in from behind her, pushing the girl's backside so hard that she bounced right back into the air. In a fluid motion Pecehssa snagged the human in her arms, cradling her with a powerful arm behind her back and another hooked behind her knees. Without losing a second of momentum, she continued forward to the mushrooms near the back of the tunnel, and the two women shared a smile while they travelled.

Though Alena was embarrassed over her slip-up, it wasn't the reason for her blush. Credit for that went to the embrace that carried her the rest of the distance.

Once they finally arrived at the makeshift waterfall, Pechessa's tail slithered outward once more, entwining around one of the more modest-sized mushrooms just underneath the base and bending it forward, giving them a bit of shelter underneath the downpour. Not enough that they didn't get any rain, of course, but just enough so they could share a moment of intimacy.

One they reached their destination, Alena was quick to unfold from Pechessa's arms, but only because she knew she wasn't going far. The snake woman had bent her lower half in such a fashion that it afforded a place for the human to sit just underneath her waistline, bringing Alena into what could generously be called her lap. As Alena shifted into position, her legs spread and she mounted her friend's tail, resting belly-to-belly with the woman while her arms slowly moved forward.

"M'lsss~" the word was a gentle coo now, and one that Alena savored when

spoken by the sweet accent of her friend. While her hands drifted towards Pechessa's face, she allowed her thumbs to hook against the sides of her hood, sweeping it back to reveal the chocolate braids framing her face and the rest of her chubby, adorable features. The word of affection was still on Pechessa's lips by the time Alena hung her arms around her shoulders and leaning forward without warning or hesitation to press a kiss firm against the other's lips.

Pechessa was a mighty creature whose origins that Alena might never even know, and yet...the serpent woman was utterly helpless when she felt the increasingly familiar lips of the human on her own, pressed in a chaste moment of pleasure that the two relished in. Pechessa was left so delighted that she couldn't even control the muscles at the very end of her tail, forcing her to shake the mushroom cap she was holding above them and giving them a sudden shower of fresh rainwater. It was enough to break their kiss amidst a shared spread of laughter, the two women peeling apart from one another with heavy blushes and rising delight.

"You're so sweet," Alena murmured. Herforehead nudged Pechessa's and rubbed back and forth with building affection. Her hands were fidgeting with joy as they explored everything she could reach - from the slender gold rings holding Pechessa's braids in place to the plump cheeks of her dear, dear friend. She was burning in the space between an emotional outburst of passion and an excitement she had only just started to explore, and everything within her from purity to sensuality was directed entirely on the other woman. "Can...can we stay here all day today? I know we should go back to foraging, but...I just want to spend it here with you."

"Cosssa, tol retta," came the whispered reply, complete with a hard nuzzle of Pechessa's forehead and another half-stolen kiss at the corner of her lips. The language barrier between them persisted and would likely never truly go away, but it didn't matter. They understood one another just fine, and for two glorious months, they had been living a life of companionship and joy.

And, for a solid three weeks by that point, one of love.

Alena wasn't entirely sure just how it happened, but...things had built between them from the very first second the serpent handed Alena her glasses. Pechessa kept her safe within the cave, and Alena knew enough about farming to help her friend survive in that harsh place, but the fondness the two held for each other stemmed deeper than those shared interests. Every time Pechessa slipped a flower into Alena's hair, every time Alena fell asleep within the protective coils of the mighty serpent, every exchanged glance and every whispered sweetness between them… Alena couldn't even quite pinpoint the day their friendship evolved into something more. In a way, it felt like it had been from the first second they set eyes on one another.

And she was *deeply* content in the idea that for the rest of her days, Pechessa would be the only person she'd need concern herself with.

The two women giggled against one another as their affection underneath the mushroom cap continued, Alena's hands growing more and more bold while Pechessa's tail writhed underneath her. Gentle explorations turned to something more focused and determined as human fingers tugged at the loose straps of Pechessa's hooded robe and the chubby serpent dug her fingers against the buttons of Alena's shirt. Bit by bit, flesh was exposed between the pair while their lips danced across the other's face, Alena making it a point to press kisses of equal joy on each of her love's cheeks just as Pechessa traced the other girl's freckles with her lips.

Little was whispered between the two as the layers of cloth were left exposed, both shirt and robe alike soon hanging open so warm flesh could be pressed together. The curves of the farmgirl were a joy to behold but Pechessa's figure was thicker and softer, practically glowing with a blush as their affection grew. With bare breasts held against one another and their bodies still half-dampened from the sporadic rainfall above, Alena finally broke the silence between them while matching their gazes and palming Pechessa's cheeks.

"You mean so much to me," the girl whispered, throat tightening and emotions overtaking her. If ever it was clear that Pechessa could understand her meaning, it was in moments like this when she fell quiet and watched the human with adoring, fond eyes. "Waking up beside you every morning...going to sleep at night curled up against you...I haven't worried about a thing since we first met." She dipped forward to suddenly break their eye contact, just so she could wrap her arms around Pechessa and give her a mighty, fierce bear hug. With their bodies closer than ever and her face buried against one of those chocolate braids, Alena let her voice creep from the back of her throat with a genuine, sincere tone. "I love you so much, Pechessa."

"Alena…" It was one of the few common tongue words the serpent had ever learned. She returned the embrace with equal fervor. With eyes closing briefly and body quaking with passion, she drew in a long, deep breath that slowly shuddered from her as emotion and excitement started to blend together. "Ronsssel, trai yetta ssslen."

As always, they didn't need the same language to understand the meaning.

The embrace between the two intensified before it started to shift, Alena's mouth creeping across Pechessa's cheek as her legs began to loosen their hold. She could already feel something pressing against her - a sensation that was becoming all the more natural as her time with Pechessa continued. The serpent woman had an impressive length that slipped out from in between her scales in moments of excitement just like this, a perfect marriage of her two halves showcased in glorious fashion. As with so many things about Pechessa, its existence was a bit of a mystery to Alena, but as always, such intrigues only pulled her in further. As soon as she could feel it pressing against her pants, the human woman gave a tiny gasp against her lover's cheek, and she slid her hands down to her own waistline to begin easing out of them.

At that point, the pleasures of each other's body had become old hat to the pair, and Pechessa knew to hold the human up by the rear while she worked one of her legs free of her pants. The entire time Alena hustled to strip, the two kept their mouths particularly close, sharing breaths and giggles before the moment she was finally freed. With her boots still on and her pants clinging to a single leg, Alena slipped right back down onto her friend's lap, though this time, that growing length was pressed flush against her entrance and begging permission.

"So excited this morning…" It wasn't clear whether Alena was talking about the serpent, or herself. It would already be their third time today, after all, but such was the way of young love. While her hands moved up and around the firm shoulders of the other woman, she started to lift her hips forward, just enough to give the tip of that glistening member a chance to line against her. While the two continued to giggle and blush, she finally allowed herself to descend, and in one fluid, practiced motion, she invited every inch of Pechessa within her.

The serpent hissed deep from the back of her throat, and the mushroom cap above them once more shook from the weight of her trembling tail. Pleasure danced across the pair in equal measure as her length was engulfed in the warmth of that sweet human, and Pechessa soon darted her head forward to once more squeeze their lips together in a rapidly growing heat.

Lovemaking between the pair was slow and tender. The gentle motions of the human's hips and the constant pressure of their breasts held taut together, the fawning caresses over each other's figure, and the kisses that seemed endless in passion and affection. The taste of her serpent lover was becoming an ever-increasing addiction for Alena, and she never tasted sweeter than while that throbbing, thick length was deeply wedged within her. As a lover, Pechessa was never selfish or cold, never distant, cruel, or rough. A far cry from any affection the man she was once promised to would ever give her, and a far cry from any joy Alena suspected any woman in her family ever knew.

It was there, in the lap of a 'monster,' that she experienced more love and joy than she ever thought she deserved...and it was no wonder that she was quite content to have the caves all to themselves for the rest of their days.

For Pechessa's part, the feeling seemed most certainly mutual. Shrouded in mystery without even rumors of her kind to inform Alena's perceptions of her, she was a creature of endlessly unique captivation. Her mighty tail. Her thick physique. Her smooth, naturally-glistening member. There was so much about Pechessa that Alena didn't know, but what she did made all the difference in the world. Far below the Feral Hills, the two had found themselves a paradise, pleasure and love merged together in a way that neither ever thought possible.

Pechessa's tail continued to gently shake the mushroom high above them, and every time it did, more rainwater from above fell across their half-naked, entwined forms. Though sometimes the cold water sent them into shivers, it only pushed them closer together, with Alena's hips rocking back and forth with renewed vigor and Pechessa tightening her hands upon her love's arms. Alena's glasses fogged up, and chilly water danced long lines across Pechessa's curvy form, and still, the two refused to separate. Tongues intertwined in a seemingly-endless dance, the human's hips continued to rock back and forth, and the union between human and monster showed no sign of stopping.

It was hard for Alena to tell just how long they remained like that. Minutes? Hours? The time made little difference, considering the bliss that flooded her. Their tender lovemaking kept going in gently rising and ebbing waves, with some moments of swifter thrusting leading into others of a passive pleasure where she simply resting on Pechessa's member and held it within her. Their lips never strayed further than a quarter inch apart, and rainwater that fell from above when they first began was still trapped in between their breasts, caught in a prison of flesh on flesh. Alena's climaxes came softly and swiftly and without exhaust - thighs trembling, breath catching in her throat, and muscles tightening around that throbbing length. She quivered gently against her love's body, and every time she came, Pechessa endeavored to hold her tighter, crushing their figures against one another while she murmured sweet words in a mysterious language against her lips.

It was when Pechessa herself finally hit her peak that the moment truly hit a new high, and once more, Alena was gifted to know what it felt like to accept the flood of her lover's cream. Breathing heavier and heavier, the serpent pushed herself to the limit within Alena's folds, and when it finally arrived, she unleashed a noise that sounded like a desperate, frightened yelp. Her entire body quaked, and the mushroom cap above shook, and those hundreds of pounds of pure snake muscle violently trembled and twitched.

And while they did, Alena simply held her beloved close, threaded fingers down her chocolate hair, and whispered hotly against her plump lips. "That's it, love...everything...give me everything," she begged and kissed Pechessa again and again in chaste and doting fashion, rubbing their noses together and encouraging her further. Even as she felt the serpent's cream flood her nethers, even as she felt the overflow pool against her thighs, even as her own body began to quiver in release, she continued to layer whisper after whisper onto her beloved's lips. "It feels so wonderful...so warm...so perfect..."

Even after all their time spent together, Pechessa was still shy. Shy about her unique body and shy about the moment of climax within her human mate. The sweet words that flowed to her soon brought the serpent's eyes to open, and she gazed at Alena with a heavy blush upon her cheeks and a gentle misting of tears within her eyes. Satisfied, pleased, and emotional.

"You're perfect," Alena was quick to whisper, pressing her palms to Pechessa's cheeks and kissing her again, and again, and again. Feather-soft moments of affection, drawing more and more emotions from the raw and trembling creature. "You're perfect. And you're mine. And I'm yours. And this is all ours."

"A...Alena...m'lsss," Pechessa purred in glowing delight and basked in the adoration of her human love. With Alena's filled entrance drawn tight around her and the heat between them at their peak, the serpent drew a deep and intensely satisfied breath. This treasure from above spoke a strange language, had no tail, and was so very, very small compared to her. And yet...it seemed that she was all Pechessa needed to be happy for all her days.

And Alena, who had forgotten so many useful items when she first ran away, who had abandoned her rucksack on her first night out, never needed any of those things to begin with. She didn't need anything from the surface. Nothing from her farm, nothing from the Homestead, and nothing from her old life.

All she needed was the love of the serpent, and the glow of the underground mushrooms.

From peril to pleasure, from isolation to connection, from a fear of snakes to an undeniable fondness of them. Such was Alena's story as you sit there and listen, enjoying your complimentary drink and all the subsequent refills. While Glory talks, the enthusiasm she shows in her storytelling is obvious - from the wild hand gestures to the attempts to speak in different voices, from the bombastic yells that fill the bar to the honestly obscene hand gestures at the spicier parts. The dwarf is a natural storyteller, but beyond that, a welcoming hostess.

You can already tell by the time her story is complete - this is a fine tavern to spend the hours in. With so many different people from all across Rugget, there's no limit to the potential friends that could be made here, just as there's no limit to the stories that Glory's most likely picked up over the years. As the kindly dwarf refills your mug one more time before heading to tend to the other patrons, she offers you a broad, warm smile and a playful wink.

"Stick around for a while longer; I'll be back to check on ya in a bit," she offers in that inviting voice, sliding the mug right back into your hand. "Just be careful to drink it down slow, alright? Or you might find yourself tripping through the woods chased by gnolls yourself, and I doubt it'll go quite as well for ya!"

With a polite smile and a toast, you turn back to your beverage and the rest of the crowd beyond the bar. There's good people to be found here - that, you can already tell. After all, they all obviously had the good sense to spend their evenings in the finest bar in Rugget, being served by the staff of the most charming hostess around.

The Most Precious Treasure is More Treasure

The night crowd at Glory's Hole roars in applause, and all because of you.

The barmaids cheer and clap, and all because of you.

The Daru bouncer forcefully throws a sneaky bastard out the door, sending them crashing into a pile of trash all the way on the other end of the street...and all because of you.

"Good eye, Meat." As the bouncer walks back to her post, she closes her fingers in a loose fist and gives you a tiny bump on the shoulder. It's meant as a playful and even friendly gesture, but it's still heavy enough to give you a jostle from your stool, forcing you to resettle and collect yourself. As you watch the mountain of a woman walk back

to the front door of the tavern, a few of the various waitstaff pass a smile along your way - not to mention a flirtatious wink or two.

It was the sign of a good establishment when the employees were just as protective of it as the owner.

The man face-down in the garbage outside had almost gotten away with it. With how busy the bar was, surely he expected nobody would notice when he scooped his hand deep into the tip jar and helped himself to a handful of gold. Whether his intention was to buy a few extra drinks or take that gold to another, lesser bar in town was unknown. Thankfully, he didn't get the opportunity to do either because of your quick eyes and a side whisper to one of the bartenders.

Your second hour at Glory's Hole, and already a local hero with the staff.

"You know, I ***almost*** *wouldn't have minded if he just would've stuffed his hand in the bar's bank, instead." The voice that draws your attention is the black-braided dwarf that ran the place, smiling as she steps up to your table yet again and invites herself to hop onto the opposite stool. In a single broad hand, she carries two mugs of one of the bar's finest ale, an aromatic drink with mysterious spices that she modestly named Glory's Glory. As she scoots one of them over and helps herself to the other, the dwarf arches her brow and gives a little chuckle. "But that's the staff's gold, and I'm not going to tolerate good help getting mistreated."*

As she raises her mug of ale in a casual toast, you clink your glass to hers and take a long, thirsty drink. A good flavor. A bracing aftertaste. A warm, satisfied feeling in the belly. Almost a shame there aren't more desperate drunks trying to make a quick coin.

"We don't really see much of that 'round these parts," Glory is quick to dismiss any silent wishes of a free exchange of heroics for drinks, chuckling as she gulps down a mouthful of her glory. "Most of the thieves in Clover stay away from the adventurer taverns, probably on account of all the people that know how to handle themselves in a fight. Hell, we don't even run into trouble with the Hoard Horde, and they're the only ones good enough to get away with it."

When the name's dropped, you tilt your head in inquisitive fashion. The Hoard Horde was a name that made its way to your ears even during your short time in Clover - even if nothing of substance was ever said about it. From what you could tell, they were more folklore than active crime syndicate, although whispers were always in the air about some grand heist they managed to pull off. Expensive tapestries, rare and magical gems, thousands of pieces of gold from the most protected vaults in town - all whisked away by the mysterious band of brigands.

"I've never had a problem with them here." Glory shrugged and leaned back on the stool while bracing herself for another drink. "Could be that they respect me as a local legend myself!" After a sudden laugh, she gestures down to the drink you're holding. "Or...much more likely, they know the only stuff I have worth stealing is best shared right from the tap, maybe while listening to a story told by a new friend."

There she went again. Always happy for an excuse. Always eager to spin a tale. As you take another gulp of Glory's Glory, that warm feeling fills your belly and settles deep down inside. With brew this fine, company like the cheerful dwarf, and the way grateful staff keep teasing the back of your hair with their fingers, there are be worse ways to spend an evening than sitting right there and listening to a tale.

Clover was a bustling city filled with all sorts of people, but only a rare few ever walked down the alley behind the cobbler's storeroom. It was a far distance away from any of the main paths taken by visitors and residents alike, pushed near the southern border of the city where the rocky coastline started to take over, as far on the fringes of Clover as one could get while still being technically within its boundaries. Even the cobbler himself nearly never went that far out of his way, and a quick peek inside would reveal stacks of boxes covered with dust so dense, it could be measured by the inch of thickness.

And as rare as visitors were to the storeroom, the alley behind was even more ignored save for the members of the Hoard Horde.

"Did good," Brass, a human, said. He was bald, big, and as broad as two dwarves standing side by side. One eye was permanently closed thanks to a long scar stretching from above his brow to below his chin, giving his half-offered gaze as much presence as his direct, forceful, inelegant words. "Boss happy. Boss reward."

"Looks like you're one of us now, rookie," Silver, a half-Daru, added. White-hair was pulled into a high-sitting ponytail, though her features were hard to place an age to. Though she lacked the height of her Daru half, the muscle tone was certainly there; not even the slightly baggy burglar's clothes could hide it. "And being one of us comes with some...perks."

"Hyaaa~" Coppers, an elf, chimed in. Even less verbose than Brass, she mostly just giggled and cackled through her day. Bright orange hair hung in a shaggy mess around her head with the points of her ears sticking out wide. Almost always carrying the scent of cinder and ash, she brought it in close while she wrapped her arms around the rookie and squeezed. "Geeeheheehe!"

And finally...the rookie. Human. With arms and stomach exposed, he wore a navy vest that flowed right up into a hood, and underneath, a mask that covered his face up to the bridge of his nose. A unique outfit, and one that branded him almost instantly as a member of Clover's underbelly, but then, considering his company, that was of no real concern. The only thing that mattered was that he did his job well, and that much had already been proven.

"Happy to oblige." The rookie helped himself to wrapping his arm around Coppers, giving her a tiny squeeze in return. The four of them were headed down the alley past the cobbler's storeroom, and although he didn't know the destination, he trusted the others. After the second story work he just did and the skill he proved to have? They'd have been mad to betray him now and lose his talents in the gang. "So, this means I'm in the HH?"

"Mostly," Silver answered, a brow lifting as she moved a hand to Coppers' back. She peeled the giggling elf away from the new boy and nudged her forward to keep them moving. Soon, they came to a halt just above a stone slab on the ground, far out of sight of any possible interlopers and deeply hidden in the shadows of the buildings on either side. While Brass knelt down to grasp the slab from the sides, Silver claimed the rookie's attention, folding her arms across her chest while she spoke. "Let's see...we've told you the rules. We've told you the punishments. We've told you what we expect from you."

The rookie nodded his hooded head. He had been in gangs that were worse, and the rules offered up were easy to agree to. The Hoard Horde were thieves, and while they absolutely excelled at it, they didn't break into other lines of work. No mercenary dealings. No assassinations. No shakedowns of the good people of Clover. No fraternizing with Cross' goons from the Homestead. They were a small, elite group that went about their business with the utmost skill and proficiency - undeniably best thieves on the entire continent of Rugget. And now, he was a part of them.

"So...I guess that just means one thing," he observed and looked down at the spot where Brass had finally pulled away the heavy stone slab. It led to a set of stairs dimly lit by a dull-burning torch, inviting him to head down into the true underbelly of Clover. He took a deep breath, steeling himself within his hood and mask. "Meeting *her.*"

Brass, Silver, and Coppers all stood side by side, regarding their newest recruit with different expressions. For Brass, the nearly emotionless gaze of a gigantic brute. Coppers wore the manic, giggling, twitching gaze of an elf that mixed one too many volatile potions. And for Silver, the smug, self-satisfied look of their leader, who gestured for the rookie to descend.

"We'll be right behind you," she promised, as if there was any doubt. "Prepare yourself, fledgling. You're about to have a welcoming party like you've never imagined."

***

Out to the cobbler's storeroom. Through a long, dark alley. Below a heavy stone slab and down a set of rickety, creaking steps. And then, through a tunnel that would've been *much* less hospitable if guests weren't expected. While the rookie led the way, he could tell – that the narrow tunnel leading to *her* was filled with traps, all of which had been disarmed for the introduction party. With every step, he could see dart slots on the wall or nearly invisible tripwires or arcane stones half-covered in dirt, daring someone to step on them. And when it came to traps in a place like this, he knew that for every one he saw, there were a dozen he didn't. This tunnel was nothing short of a deathtrap, and yet the four of them moved through it completely unharmed, all because they were of the precious few permitted entry.

Once the rookie made his way to the clearing at the end of the tunnel, he could see the reason for the security. "It...it's...oh, by Doce's dice…"

The only time a thief in Sombfal was ever religious was when they were about to die or gazing at a pile of treasure so massive that they were sure they already did. Even with the mask and hood, there was no hiding the shock overtaking him, eyes as wide as saucers while he beheld the largest mountain of treasure he had ever seen in his entire life. Hell, the largest he had ever heard about. A bounty that would put a dragon to shame and enough to make any thief's heart leap in delight...even if he knew acting uncouth towards it would lead to a swift end. It'd almost be worth it to say for a fleeting fraction of a second such a bounty was in part his own.

Piles of gold twice as tall as the rookie's head. Gems and jewelry and marble rods set with silver plating, potions of swirling red and blue, and paintings made by some of history's finest artists now casually leaned against mountains of opulence. It was such a glorious display that even the most innocuous items in the pile no doubt had some deeper value or purpose, from a pair of leather boots to a wrought iron mask laying casually atop one of the smaller heaps. It was a celebration of wealth, and sitting right there in the center of it all was a massive wooden chest that naturally drew the rookie's gaze.

The thief couldn't possibly know the true importance of that chest, but there was no denying the glory of it. Preserved sandalwood reinforced with gold and stylized to be a work of art unto itself, with large, fist-sized rubies lining the corners and jade strips along the top surface. At the very center of that bathtub-sized treasure chest was something truly unique that the rookie had never seen in all his years of rampant theft: a face built into the front like the maidenhead of a ship. Crafted from the finest ivory, it depicted a beautiful woman with long tresses of hair affixed with aquamarines. A single red ruby was perched at the front of her forehead just before a polished bronze crown was set above her head. She rested there with one eye closed and the other covered by a weathered eyepatch, and on close inspection, the rookie could see that even it was built into the framework of the chest and made from an old strip of leather that was of the finest quality. Seshani bear hide, if he wasn't mistaken.

The thief found his way moving to the edge of the chest, utterly captivated by the sight of it. His eyes were large and his mouth agape underneath his mask, admiring the thing not only for the work of artistry it was but the fact that it doubtless held unfathomable treasures within. Surrounded by as much glittering gold as it was, the contents of the chest *had* to be the sort of thing that would pluck most greedy men's souls from their body.

Before his avarice got the best of him, the rookie looked over his shoulder and gazed towards Brass, Coppers, and Silver. He didn't dare so much as rest a hand atop the chest itself, though he did linger close to it, feeling a natural pull towards something of such tremendous value and beauty. Still, he was there in the depths of their hideout for a reason...and his curiosity was only growing the longer he lingered in this trove.

"Do we...wait here for her?" he asked, tilting his head while gazing at the trio. Brass' face was the usual mask of stalwart defiance while Coppers was giggling to herself, and Silver merely wore a smug smile. None of them immediately answered him, and it made the thief shift uncomfortably on a heel. Usually, unexpected silence among rogues meant that the daggers would be flying before too long. "Say something. Where is she? Does she even exist? What is all this?"

"Should we teeeeell him?" Coppers shifted back and forth, half-bunkering behind Silver while she grinned. Lurking in the shadow of the half-Daru made her look all the more slender and sneaky, especially when she rubbed her hands together in mischievous glee. "I'm so excited, Silver! So, so, so!"

"Wait," Brass barked out, voice low and steady and firm. "Not ruin boss' fun."

"After what the rookie managed to bring us, she'll have enough fun as is." It was Silver that finally spoke out in defense of the rookie, and she pulled a hand down to a small pouch hanging from her side. Fishing from it a flawless, clear gemstone that danced with light as soon as it was surrounded by the gold all around them, Silver held it upward in full view, pinched between two fingers and twisting it gently from side to side. "L'wain's Eye, exactly where it was supposed to be. The new guy did a great job, Boss, and didn't try to screw us over. He's got my vote."

"Hrm." Brass was swift to nod and make a noise that could be discerned as affirmative, throwing in his agreement. Despite the fact that the rookie couldn't see who they were addressing, their words were enough to calm his senses and take a bit of the edge off. Assassinations didn't usually come after confessions of skill and talent.

"Mine tooooo!" Coppers giggled, at that point practically hanging on Silver. She had climbed up the half-Daru's back and was resting her chin on the older woman's silver-maned head, staring at the rookie and the chest before her. While she swivelled back and forth, Silver barely flinched, relying on her more durable Daru blood to let her be a fitting elf jungle gym. "He did good! No killin'! No backtalk! And I bet he's super cute behind the mask!" She paused long enough to whisper to Silver, although when she did it her voice was loud enough that everyone could hear, "I don't *really* think that, but I'm trying to be nice!"

"Heh. Good job, Coppers," Silver chuckled in the aftermath, before shaking her head and holding up the gem once more. "That's all our votes, Boss. What's the final word?"

As she asked it, Silver suddenly and unexpectedly threw the gem that the rookie had stolen, tossing it straight towards the mighty chest in the center of the room. It came so quick that the rookie didn't have a chance to catch it, but he quickly realized it didn't matter. In the split-second before the gem crashed against the surface of that ornate chest, the lid opened up of its own volition, and it landed on a bed of golden coins that gently broke its fall.

What happened next sent the rookie stumbling backward, eyes wide and heart racing while he tumbled towards the others. He would've fallen flat on his backside if it wasn't for Silver's powerful hands catching his shoulders, holding him steady and offering him a tiny smirk while they watched. Gripped by the half-Daru, the rookie became witness to something only a scant few in Clover ever saw. The guild mistress of the Hoard Horde. The cursed queen of the Clover seas. The Boss.

"Ohh, he truly did a fine job, didn't he?" The voice that filled the air was sensual and slow, spoken from the lips of the ivory face built into the front of the chest. As it spoke, that single eye slowly drifted open to behold the four thieves before it - the three loyal long-term members and the fourth that had come to join their family. While the chest's gaze fell upon them all, her ivory smile grew, and with a soft shuffling of her frame, the fanciful gem dipped underneath the gold it landed on. "L'wain's Eye, my my my! I've wanted to add this to my collection for years. Such a fine, sweet young man to help an old woman out…"

The rookie was still staring in dumbstruck awe by the time Silver shoved him from behind, pressing a hand to his back and thrusting him forward. Fidgeting within his unique robed vest, leaving his arms exposed to show the goosebumps on his flesh, he looked directly into the chest's face and spoke with a tone heavy on respect. He didn't quite understand just *what* the guild mistress was, but she clearly deserved his most polite tone.

"A pleasure to add to such an impressive trove, m'lady." He bowed from the waist, addressing her like she was a noble of the finest breeding and not a bizarre, animated treasure chest. "Though might I say, nothing I'd uncover above the surface would compete with the artistry and glory of the magnificence before me."

Corny. Flattering. True. People didn't endeavor to join the Horde Hoard unless they had a keen eye for treasure and could appreciate it beyond the greedy, avaricious impulses of others. The trove, the tunnel, the alley, the cobbler's storeroom...they all led to a place where only the finest eyes could enjoy the finest of bounties. The rookie was one of them now, and his words made the chest rumble with grand, delighted laughter.

"Ha! And what an addition you'll be, boy!" The ivory face on the front of the chest beamed, her eye flashing as she levelled her gaze upon him. "Welcome aboard. I think I'll call you...Mercury."

And with that, the rookie had a name. The rookie had a boss. The rookie had a new family, one that was eager to celebrate his arrival.

"Ooh, ooh, Boss! Boss, Boss, Boss!" Coppers lurched forward on Silver's shoulders, raising her hand and waving it back and forth. "Does this mean we can have a welcoming party?! Please, please, please?!"

"We *just* had a successful heist celebration party two days ago," Silver laughed, although judging by her tone, she didn't seem particularly opposed.

"Yeah, but...but now we have Mercury!" Coppers giggled as she turned her gaze back to the boss. "Pleeeeaaaase?"

The mature, ivory-chiselled face of the chest looked at the energetic elf, and once more rumbled with the sound of delight. Her voice was throaty and even a bit hoarse like that of any weathered pirate, though there was a constant joy in almost everything she said. Easily the finest guild leader that

Mercury had ever known, something he was confident in saying even having just met her.

"A welcoming party it is!" she announced, and amidst Coppers' enthusiastic cheering, she levelled her gaze towards the newest member of their family. Her words were clear and loud to still be heard over Coppers' frantic giggling, but even then...Mercury wasn't sure he heard her right the first time. "Get the pants off, boy. It's time to show you how the Hoard Horde celebrates."

"...sorry, what?"

***

"He's so in love with treasure that he'd fuck it if he could" was a phrase often spoken about Mercury, just as it had been spoken about countless other thieves over history. It was the sort of thing murmured around poker tables for a surefire laugh, often spoken by those that had no idea just how real of a possibility it was.

No one that ever made that jest had been a member of the Hoard Horde or been privy to the pleasures of one of their grand celebrations.

At first, the newly-appointed Mercury was in awe at what he was witnessing. The mountains of gold that surrounded the guild mistress started to shift and take form, moving to swarm around her like a sentient wave moving of its own volition. He soon pieced together that the vault at the end of the tunnel wasn't just a pile of treasure with a talking chest so much as it was the hiding spot for this remarkable creature - a flawless presence that controlled every bit of loot added to her form and was able to manifest the reach of her wealth in a very physical, tangible fashion.

While Mercury watched, the tiny elf Coppers was plucked from the shoulders of Silver, and her giggling figure was hoisted up by a tendril made of hundreds of gold coins that had forged themselves into a tentacle. Grasping Coppers by the ankle, it dangled the playful elf upside down while other, smaller fingers of gold rushed up towards her, plucking at the buttons of her tunic and helping to expose her slender, small-chested frame.

Mercury's attention was then drawn to Brass, the towering figure who moved to take a spot beside the chest. He was practically wading through a sea of treasure by now that rolled well past his knees and towards his waist, and Mercury could see that already, those tendrils were pawing at his crotch while he moved, teasing and fondling a growing bulge. When the bald brute of a man drew near, there was a sudden weight that crashed around him with so much force that it would've floored any weaker soul - but Brass merely caught it against his chest and held it there. While Mercury's eyes widened further, he could see - the coalesced grouping of hundreds of coins were taking the vague shape of a woman's lower half, complete with legs wrapped around Brass' shoulders as he buried his face against where a golden slit might lie.

Of the other veterans, only Silver moved with any level of patience. While she passed Mercury, she didn't hesitate to clap the boy on the back, chuckling as she brought her elegant, muscular figure over to the edge of the chest. She knelt right there before the ivory face of the guild mistress and drew her fingers down to caress the cheek of the sculpture, just before dipping forward to press a slow, surprisingly tender kiss upon her lips. While Mercury played the role of the spectator, Silver kissed her employer for a long and lingering moment, and the intimacy between the two was so great that even the chest's single eye drifted close to savor it. Even while it did, the rest of her bounty continued to shift around them, swinging Coppers from side to side and further pooling around Brass. When the kiss between the guild leader and Silver finally ended, the half-Daru woman stood and dropped her hands to the edges of her loose-fitting outfit so she could slowly strip it away.

"You don't get to watch for much longer without joining in, Mercury." She smiled at the boy watching from the sidelines and let a small grin play upon her features. "We're not here to give you a peepshow, unless you're planning on paying for admission."

"Don't tease him, Silver. He'll join whenever he's ready," the guild mistress herself spoke up with a large grin drawing on her face and her eye narrowing upon the young man. While she did so, something started to shift right before Mercury's eyes, and rising from a gold-covered floor emerged another figure for display. Once more, she had pulled her glittering coins together into a somewhat human-like shame, this time that of a woman's backside on her knees with her rump presented. It wiggled back and forth and showcased two particularly noticeable spots for the young man to jam his length, not to mention a pair of wide hips and a plump gold-sculpted rear for him to hold onto while he did it. While the guild mistress offered him a taste of her pleasure, she finally looked back to Silver and purred in delight as the half-Daru finally finished stripping. "As lovely as always. In you go!"

Suddenly, Silver was sent to a fit of laughing as a wave of gold crashed against her from behind, lifting the impressively muscular woman up into the air only to send her crashing harmlessly into the chest itself. She sunk into it as smoothly as bathwater and stretched out much the same, her silver hair bouncing around her head as she got comfortable with a heavy, throaty sigh. Easing down up to her bustline, the woman shuddered in bliss while she settled in, licking her lips and giving the young cadet another playful look.

"You...couldn't even imagine what you're missing," she murmured, her cheeks already flushing. When she swung a hand out from the surface of the chest and to the mountain of treasure beyond, she flashed him a pleased look with just a hint of guarded possessiveness. "The mistress' trove is our playground, Mercury. Have as much fun as you like. Just...not here." She drummed the edges of the chest with her hands, claiming that sacred spot as her own. "This is *my* seat."

The guild mistress herself merely chuckled, and whatever she did to Silver below the surface of the gold sitting inside of her was enough to make the powerhouse of a woman blush. Intensely.

Rogues were usually the quiet type, and Mercury was no different. This, however, might have been the first time he was silent out of sheer awe and admiration rather than any professional interest. From side to side, he gazed at the celebration before him, starting where Brass was firmly burying his mouth against the golden mound pressed against him. While he doted on the mistress with oral delights that Mercury couldn't even begin to understand, the mistress was rewarding him by pooling her treasure up to his waist. Tendrils of gold were kneading at his bulge while even more of it was creeping upward, slipping down the front of his pants to massage a massive length in what seemed to be a gentle, affectionate grip.

His attention towards Brass was soon peeled by the rabid giggling of Coppers, by now swinging overhead like a chandelier. She was stripped naked and holding a glorious crown atop her head, one that Mercury instantly recognized as being a pilfered treasure that made waves in the local thief circles a few months prior. Seemed it was the Hoard Horde all along that ransacked the Clover history museum and made off with the relics of legacies past.

"Heeeee, look at me! I'm Queen Coppers, and my pussy is the royal courtyard!" Coppers laughed in her spastic style while she dangled, and her words naturally forced Mercury to look to her nethers. As she dangled upside-down it seemed like the mistress had taken to stuffing the elf's holes with a few lavish rods of beautiful craftsmanship. After all, any thief knew that there was nothing quite like an overflowing loot sack! Judging by the noises that Coppers was making, it sounded like she agreed.

When Mercury turned back to Silver, it was indeed evident that even her attention was no longer upon him. With her body stretched out and the gold inside of the mistress' chest rising up to her bustline, she was convulsing in what was likely the first climax of the party. Her eyes were rolled back in her head, her mouth open and tongue dangling forward, and she just barely managed to move her hands to the edges of the chest to hold on. She was actively trembling in her seat while the layer of coins on the surface shimmered and shook, letting Mercury know that whatever was going on was vigorous, fierce, and *just* what Silver wanted. Judging by the smug smile on the mistress' mono-eyed, ivory face, she was delighting in delivering it.

Finally, Mercury's attention spun down to the offering he was given: that amorphous lower half of a woman, stuck out from the ooze-like river of coins that surrounded them. It wiggled back and forth to continue inviting him forward and one of the vault's armored gauntlets suddenly emerged from underneath, pressing fingers against the sides of what could be considered its slit, and spreading itself all the further.

Mercury blinked, tilted his head, and took a fierce breath to brace himself while his hands dropped to the front of his pants. If this madness was truly the way the greatest thieves of Clover celebrated, then he would be proud to join them.

A family of bandits was only as strong as their bond, after all.

***

It was remarkable just how...natural it felt, having his length gripped by an entrance made of gold coins working in perfect unison. Whether it was the magic that bound the guild mistress to this unique form or the fact that he really *did* just want to fuck treasure, Mercury found that gilded entrance inviting, warm, and even wet to slither into. While he quaked in pleasure, the coins tightened around his member to give him a tiny squeeze, and when he cast a look towards the mistress herself, that ivory face offered a small, knowing wink. With no other invitation needed, the newest member of the Hoard Horde started to pump his hips slowly back and forth, his head still spinning over the unique sensations he was experiencing.

And though it wasn't new to the trio of thieves he was joining, they were clearly nonetheless having just as much fun. The towering Brass and the giggling Coppers were both savoring their respective treatment - and in Coppers' case, continuing to swing high above them all as a mighty tendril of coalesced coins held her suspended in the air. Silver herself didn't even seem to acknowledge the others, bouncing around as she was within the mouth of the chest. Several times in rapid succession the woman's voice echoed through the vault in dynamic fashion, and every time someone cast their gaze in the direction of her eyes, they were closed, and she was practically melting deeper and deeper into the guild mistress' most intimate embrace.

Surrounded by such amazing sights and gripped in such an unconventionally inviting entrance, it wasn't long before Mercury could feel his climax rushing through him. With a heavy groan, he pushed forward to hilt himself within the golden backside offered towards him, his fingers sinking deep into the coins and grasping just like it was a flesh and blood backside. His member was spasming in delight just as a hand forged of coins slipped from the gold pooled around his knees, gently massaging his sack to help encourage him to give her every last drop he could manage. It was an effective strategy, and Mercury found himself convulsing with his eyes rolled back in his head, his member unloading squirt after squirt of rich, warm spunk into the treasures of the vault.

"Enjoying yourself, young man?" the guild mistress inquired with a gently arched brow on her ivory face. She slowly licked her lips in pointed fashion. "My my, first L'wain's Eye and now all of this? A generous one looking to earn my favor, you are!"

Mercury was grinning behind his mask, but almost completely unable to answer the guild mistress due to the sensations rolling through him. When he finally exhausted himself and dumped the last of his load into that tiny cave of gold, he flopped onto his backside, smoothly caught in a comfortable pile of glittering wealth that supported his fall and helped him to relax. There he sat, his member still sticking straight up while the hole he had just used simply faded away, merging with the rest of the hoard. To what extent the strange creature that ran the gang enjoyed his cream, Mercury couldn't possibly say, but at the very least, it seemed like she was content.

The thief slowly raised a hand to give the guild mistress a thumbs-up, along with an approving, content nod. He was a member of the Hoard Horde now, and he could already tell...the perks were going to be intensely satisfying.

"What is she?" Glory lifts a brow to your question, pursing her lips in thought. A slow, steady roll comes to her shoulders before she finally settles once more, and she clicks her tongue to the roof of her mouth. "Hard to say. She could just be a particularly old mimic that stored one too many magical items. Could be a thief cursed to take the form of something she once coveted. Although...if you want my personal guess?"

With that, the dwarf leans forward across the bar, her cleavage pressing together with such an alluring squeeze that it's actively difficult to avoid staring. Her hand drifts forward, and she points to your eye, making a sweeping motion in a circle around it.

"Her eyepatch? I think she's a former pirate. And not just any pirate, either." With a matter-of-fact nod, she leans back and settles her arms underneath her breasts again. "Some time ago, long before the first brick in this old tavern

was laid, Clover had a hell of a time dealing with some freebootin' filly named Rich Riley. She was notorious, ransacked every free spot of dockside she could, mostly going after what nobles were left after the royalty stepped down. And just like the gang today, they didn't kill. Relied on skills and sneaks, and the bond she had with her crew."

If the guild mistress deep below the city was indeed the woman once known as Rich Riley, it seemed like she had perfected a way to keep her crew fiercely loyal. When you observe as much, Glory can't help but laugh, and slowly stands from the stool while she picks up the empty mugs.

"Could be, friend, could be," she muses, and flashes you a tiny wink. "But with that honest streak you've got, I doubt you'll ever make your way to meet her."

While she passes, the dwarf makes it a point to gently bump your shoulder with her hips, and when you look up, she casts you a friendly smile from over the edge of her shoulder.

"That's all right, though," she offers as consolation. "You're makin' plenty of friends up here."

Barmaids, bouncers, and the curvy, hospitable beauty that keeps throwing free drinks your way.

Tales From the Glory's Hole Gang

"Here. Try this."

You're barely able to open your mouth before Glory shoves a fork in your direction, loaded up with a large chunk of apple pie. As the flaky crust pushes against your lips, your options become desperately limited - open up your mouth and take the offered bite, or let it crumble down to the bar below and possibly offend your hostess. After taking the only wise option and parting your lips for the forced treat, Glory ushers it right against your tongue before pulling the fork back and giving you a stern, scrutinizing stare.

"How is it? Is it too tart? Can you taste the cinnamon?" She folds her arms across her chest while the fork is still braced between two fingers, and she wiggles it

back and forth like the pendulum of a clock. "I ground up the skins and baked them into the filling, so it should be textured but not grainy, with just the right amount of crunch. Do you think it'd help if I added a dollop of ice cream? What about pears instead?" She pauses and rubs her chin in concentration. "I don't know if I can get a shipment of pears in time. I mean, I'm sure I can get some pears, but not good pears. Not the best pears."

You've only known Glory for three short hours, but this is a side of the dwarf that seems downright strange. Her confidence remains perfectly in check, but it's tempered by a perfectionist focus that seems almost...worried when set against her normal tone. From the second you entered the tavern, it was clear that Glory was in charge of everything she surveyed, and this pie-insecurity is an odd fit. When you take a bite and press the issue, the curvy, braided woman gives a small chuckle and rubs idly at the back of her head.

"Caught me fussing, yeah?" she smirks, and tosses the fork casually to the table before drumming the fingers of both hands across it. "Just not much of a baker. I try, of course - my dads are two of the best cooks back in Rustpad Basket. And it's a family tradition that a job well done gets rewarded with a real feast. I'm expectin' that I'll have to put one together in a few days, myself."

You don't even have to speak - the look on your face upon realizing Glory's sentimental side is enough to make the dwarf laugh. When she leans back against the rear bar, it's with enough weight from her lovely backside that the bottles behind her gently rattle, and she squares her eyes upon you with a look flirting between playfully defensive and coy. It looks like this is a side of her she isn't always forthcoming with...but doesn't resent the opportunity to show it.

"My staff's like my family 'round here," she smiles, broad and proud. "Some are a little more than others. One of my best is out on a recipe run for me out past Rugget, drifting near the edges of the Terro Marsh." She swiftly holds out a hand, as the mere mention of that dangerous place is enough to bring about worry and concern, even for total strangers. "It's all right, she's fine. She's always fine. That's why she's one of my best. In fact..."

Here it is. You can already tell. You settle down into your seat and almost shyly nudge your half-filled drink forward, hoping that the dwarf's natural inclination to offer free booze with every free story will implore her into motion. Sure enough, while Glory has a reminiscent look in her eyes, she smoothly picks up your mug and tips it underneath the nearest tap, filling it up while she begins.

"Let me tell ya about her last trip out. Maybe then you'll understand why she's got a special place in Glory's Hole."

You blink. She really never seems to understand how it sounded when she said stuff like that.

Across all of Sombfal, few commanded as much respect as the Stodar. Towering warriors with green skin and bodies of toned and flawless muscle, they were known for their skill in battle and their boundless, untiring power. A single Stodar Warmaster could bring an entire clan of gnolls to their knees without earning a scratch, and their mastery of unique weaponry was unmatched even by the most skilled mercenaries in the war quarter of Clover. They were mysterious, rare creatures to see among the plains of Rugget, the stuff of legend, myth, and rumor. If a Stodar was seen out in the wild it could only be assumed they were on the hunt, tracking down some target of profound importance.

And then there was Ryah.

She was different from Stodar in a lot of ways, both evident to the outside observer and in manners one could only tell by having the pleasure of interacting with her. Anyone could see that compared to others of her kind, she was tiny. Standing just a little over five feet tall compared to the mountains that were her kin, she was also far less hefty. While most Stodar stood like sturdy walls of muscle clad in strange, heavy metal armor, Ryah was dagger-thin and kept her figure almost completely hidden underneath the embrace of a black cloak that wrapped entirely around her body.

To peek underneath said cloak would reveal a slender figure gripped by the embrace of dyed purple leather with an exposed midsection showing a flat green belly and a few black straps crossing over her flesh, each one holstering a line of daggers. Each thigh was framed with a lightweight silver chainmail that didn't last long before vanishing into high-fitting leather boots, each one sporting yet another dagger in a holster for quick and easy access. The sleeves leading from her purple armor were left pitch black, snugly holding small but dense muscles in a tight embrace, and at the beginning of a pair of laced wrist cuffs, she had yet another pair of sheathes with - of course - two more daggers.

Ryah really liked daggers. So she wasn't *totally* unlike other Stodar.

Her skin was lighter than most of her kind, and instead of the deep forest green of other Stodar, she looked more like a fresh sprig of mint. Well-styled black hair framed her face with her bangs allowed to sweep down to her chin on the left side, serving to half-hide a set of well-aged scars that crossed her cheek, like those made from a slashing beast. And while most Stodar were proud to sport a pair of pronounced but short tusks from the corners of their lips, Ryah had but a single one jutting out from her right corner, the other having been long since left behind on some wild and violent adventure. Unlike most Stodar, Ryah was tiny, elegant, graceful, and quick - and in perhaps the biggest deviation from the rest of her kind, she was also friendly.

After all, being an adventurer was a dangerous job if all you did was smash, destroy, and growl.

"I got it!" Ryah was beaming by the time she hopped back on board the tiny boat docked at an island off the distant shore of Rugget. She was clutching in her hand a well-secured scroll case, bound with wax on both ends and preciously protected against the environment and tampering. "That wasn't so bad after all! The Daru were a *little* hesitant to give it up, but Mercy did a fine job of convincing them."

As she stepped back onto the deck, the rest of the tiny crew all turned to greet her with a smile. They, like Ryah herself, were part of the most elite group of adventurers in Rugget and beyond - official representatives of the country's greatest bar, Glory's Hole. Beyond Ryah herself there were four more on the deck of the ship: the heavily-armored human paladin, Mindy; the dwarven sorceress, Marcy; the elven swordsman, Murphy, and the rugged, towering, bugbear pirate, Morley. All four of the others cheered in unison as Ryah got back on board the ship, Mindy clapping her hands together as she approached.

"Great work, Ryah!" She beamed and dropped a supportive hand against Ryah's shoulder. Mindy was the tallest of the bunch outside of their bugbear team member, a brown-skinned woman with thick curls of hair and eyes that sparked with golden light from time to time. A paladin through and through, she was as brave and noble as one could be. "What about Mercy? Is she coming up behind you, lass?"

"Oh, Mercy is staying behind," Ryah responded just as she tucked the scroll case deep within the folds of her cloak and gave Mindy a simple nod. "The negotiations with the Daru were pretty tense until Mercy offered to go down on their leader, and...well, she was enjoying herself when I left. I'm sure she'll catch up."

From a crew of six down to five. No big deal, they still had plenty of party to spare!

"Well, all right!" Murphy stepped forward, flashing his most charming smile towards Ryah as he moved past her to the edge of the ship. Without any hesitation, he began to draw back up the ramp just as Mindy moved to cut the rope keeping them moored at the Daru dock. "We'll sail straightaway to Clover harbor, and we'll have Glory's treasure in her hands by morning! Morley! Raise the sails!"

"You've got it, Murphy!" the response from the bugbear followed, and Ryah watched with a broadening smile as the other four members of the crew all got to work. With the scroll case secured under her cloak and the ship finally moving once more, the Stodar woman turned on a heel to gaze out at the sea ahead.

Usually, the jobs they took on for Glory hit some sort of hurdle that slowed them down, but this time, much to Ryah's surprise, they were actually ahead of schedule! She had big hopes for this particular mission - hopes that were almost immediately squashed when she heard the voice of the dwarf Marcy chime up from behind her.

"Hey, we're making great time!" she chuckled just as she did her part to help the ship to set sail. "We 'ought to have ourselves a little party tonight to celebrate!"

From the sidelines of the ship, Ryah whimpered, and tightened her fingers around the scroll case. She enjoyed working with Mindy, Marcy, Murphy, Morley, and Mercy...but she knew enough to know that those words were usually the end of any smooth sailing they'd enjoyed up to that point.

Sure enough, by the time evening came, Ryah was laying in her bunk and staring up at the ceiling while the rest of the ship was overtaken with the sounds of revelry and passion. Mercy might not have stayed behind with the Daru had she known the sort of fun the rest were going to have without her, from Marcy singing drunken dwarven sea shanties while she and Morley had vigorous sex to how Mindy was loudly and proudly proclaiming how fiercely she was dominating Murphy. Their moans and screams pierced the air of an otherwise peaceful night at sea, so sharp that it reached Ryah all the way down in the depths of the boat.

Ryah, as always, didn't partake. Enough of their past missions had been derailed by the fuck-hungry nature of the rest of the crew, and she knew the score by now. If that precious package had any chance of making its way into Glory's deserving hands, at least *one* of them had to stay focused. Even if the others were making it a hard road to do so.

"Yes, yes, give it to meeeee!" Marcy's voice echoed through the air, dipping into a long, joyful octave before she remembered the next verse. “Ohhhh, and the boat tossed hard, but the crew was harder, yo ho, yo ho--”

“That’s it, take it! Mmm, that tight little ass of yours sure loves my fist!” Mindy’s voice cut off Marcy’s, along with a particularly desperate moan from Murphy. Morley was next to make his own thundering bugbear voice known, and when he roared with hungry passion, Marcy’s song hit a whole new peak. All four of them were on the deck of the ship, enjoying each other underneath the stars, and all four of them were utterly shameless in their fun. The very ship itself rocked from the momentum of their passion, swinging back and forth more than the waves themselves did. And down below deck, tucked into her bed but still wearing her cloak and leather armor, Ryah stared straight ahead with a sinking feeling in her stomach and an errant thought resting in the back of her mind.

“I wonder if they’re actually paying attention to where the ship is heade--”

Crash! Splintered wood, rushing water, and the sudden sound of frightened - yet still orgasmic screams - filled the air. As the ship made a hard half-landing against the rocky shoreline far north of Clover, Ryah simply sighed and stayed in bed. Her hands tightened around the waterproof scroll case she still hoped to deliver, and even as the water levels rose above her bunk and started to soak her heels, she just kept staring up at the ceiling with a deadpan, conceding expression.

“Guess it’s gonna be one of *those* missions after all.”

***

Glory would *not* be receiving her package by morning, if at all. It was five hours after the ship made an unceremonious "landing" against the jagged rocks along the coast that the crew was on the move again - minus the bugbear Morley, who offered to stay behind to guard it until they could send a recovery crew.

From a crew of five to four. No big deal, they still had plenty of party to spare!

Unfortunately, they also had no scroll case. It all happened pretty quickly after the crew crashed. The sound of the wreck drew the attention of the nearby beefolk who had built a hive not too far off, and while those buzzing, humanoid insects sure were helpful in assisting the crew by plucking them out of the water, they were *also* pretty shameless about robbing them blind. Mindy's armor, Marcy's magical staff, Murphy's sword, and Ryah's daggers were all carried off like so much pollen on a beefolk's backside along with the treasure they were still determined to deliver. And now, hours later, with the crew as feisty as they were frustrated, the four lurked behind a large rocky outcropping while they studied the beefolk hive in the near distance.

"All right, we've been down this road before," Ryah whispered, holding a stick in one hand while she drew a map in the dirt. After her words sunk in, she visibly winced and pinched the bridge of her nose. "I can't *believe* we've been down this road before."

"If you know a way to *not* wreck a ship mid-orgy and get our stuff stolen by beefolk, I'd love to hear it," Mindy chimed in, who at that point was crouching in nothing but her bra and panties. Her attire had suffered the most from the shipwreck and subsequent mugging, the downside of dressing almost entirely in beautiful, shiny armor that looked truly tempting to the segmented eyes of beefolk.

"It's just like last time, then," the dwarf Marcy chimed up, clapping her hands together and gesturing towards the elf. "We know where their treasure honeycomb is, so we'll send Murphy to distract the guards while the rest of us sneak in and steal it back."

"The three of you abandoned me last time," Murphy grumbled, scowling at the others, but Ryah was quick to counter.

"We didn't abandon you! That's not how that worked!" the Stodar snapped right back, pointing squarely at the elf's nose. "Your *exact* words were 'I'm having a lot of fun fucking these beefolk, so go on without me. I'll catch up!'"

"Then you came back all sticky," Mindy noted.

"But sweet!" Marcy quipped. "I enjoyed putting my tongue on you."

Murphy just pouted, his arms folding across his chest while the other three continued their plan. At a certain point, Mindy reached out a hand and snagged the stick away from Ryah, drawing a new line across the map and musing with a small smile tugging at the corner of her lips.

"Marcy, what if you went this way while Ryah and I hit the treasure honeycomb?" she asked. "That'll take you to their processing area. It's Spring, so you *should* be able to get some of their fresh, seasonal marigold honey. And you *know* how valuable that stuff is."

"It's Rugget's most powerful aphrodisiac," Marcy whispered, her eyes widening just before her smile started to grow. "Aside from my fat dwarven ti-"

"If we can steal a keg of that honey, it'll make Glory forget about the fact that we wrecked her boat," Ryah interrupted before correcting herself. "Again. So, I say we go for it. Is everyone in agreement?"

Ryah, Mindy, and Marcy all put their hands forward in a stack, and all three looked towards the still-pouting Murphy. The elf swordsman - so quick and clever and skilled - gave an irate huff before finally dropping his hand into the pile as he grumbled, "This time, you better not leave me behind."

"I promise we won't," the barely-clothed Mindy responded. "Unless you specifically tell us to."

The beefolk hive was quiet that early in the morning, most likely because they were all tuckered out from mugging a half-drunk, mostly-naked crew of adventurers. Thankfully, the creatures didn't live in colonies nearly as populated as those of their diminutive cousins, and each hive tended to be less than twenty beefolk rather than a swarm of thousands. It made for an accessible heist for a quick-witted crew, and when Glory's gang made their way to the target, they started to carry out their plan with an efficiency that hardly seemed capable considering the incompetence that led to them being in this situation to begin with.

Ryah, Mindy, and Marcy waited in the nearby bushes as Murphy made his approach, swaggering and smiling at the two beefolk standing guard outside the entrance to the hive. He was a lot like them - thin and gangly with a particularly narrow waist, and while he didn't have the segmented eyes, the striped thorax, or the pronounced, dangerous stinger sticking out from his backside, he still managed to carry a bee-like sway to his movements. At the same time aimless and purposeful, he sauntered up to the pair and offered them a respectful bow that dipped deep from the waist. His long tresses of silver hair nearly dusted across the ground.

"Good morning, you beautiful, graceful lovelies," Murphy's voice carried through the air, and he gazed up at the pair glaring back at him. "While you were stealing our armor and weapons and pummeling us with those tiny fists of yours, I couldn't help but wonder...how *could* we thank you from plucking us from the ocean?"

On the sidelines, Ryah, Mindy, and Marcy continued to watch from the moment Murphy swaggered to the pair of beefolk to the instant that they both looped their arms around his own, pawing at him and dragging him deeper into the hive amidst a swarm of buzzes that sounded a bit like giggling. As the trio disappeared, Ryah regarded the two women she was working with, murmuring from the very back of her throat as she braced a foot to the ground and prepared to dart forward, "I will *never* see what they see in them."

"You mean Murphy in the beefolk or the beefolk in Murphy?"

"Yes," Ryah nodded, before gesturing with a swift hand. "C'mon, let's go."

From there, the three adventurers darted forward to tackle their plan head on. Before they got within ten feet of the entrance to the hive, they could already hear the sounds of buzzing and the beating of wings. Apparently, Murphy was already hard at work appeasing the beefolk and keeping them distracted. By that point, Ryah's movements were whisper-quiet and for *once*, her position wasn't given away by her companions, thanks to Mindy's heavy, jangling armor being stolen and the paladin forced to pad around in her underwear. Following the lead of the Stodar, the other two women kept close behind her as they slithered through the entrance and quickly took a turn, following a path that they already knew through unlikely experience.

"Love how it smells in here," Mindy whispered from her point between the other two, drawing in a deep, satisfied breath and holding it for an appreciative few seconds. "Smells like--"

"Honey, Mindy. It smells exactly like honey," Marcy chirped from behind. "And if we don't get our stuff back before Murphy's done, it'll also smell like bee cum."

"I thought honey *was* bee cum."

"You have a fundamental misunderstanding about how bees work," Ryah whispered, gazing over her shoulder at the paladin. "Honey is...uh...it's..."

She looked to the bald dwarf taking up the rear, who simply shrugged. "Bee cum?"

"Bee cum."

"We're bee-cumming experts at thi-- Ow!" Mindy winced as both Ryah and Marcy stretched out a hand to punish her, the Stodar's finger flicking her nose and the dwarf simply pulling her waistband and snapping her panties.

"Shh." Ryah pressed a finger to her lips and gestured for the others to keep close behind her. The sound of Murphy's work from further down the hive continued and even sounded more pronounced as time went on. There were more wings beating and the muffled sound of deeper humming, right along with a litany of Murphy's moans that were growing in intensity. It sounded like more beefolk were joining the fun, and as the hive continued to swarm the elf like he was a walking, talking flower, the easier the job became for the others. Eventually, the three women reached an intersection set amidst the honeycombed walls, and Ryah pointed down one hall while gesturing towards Marcy.

"Okay, the honey chamber should be that way," she whispered. "Grab as much as you can quietly carry and meet us back here."

"Got it," Marcy nodded, took a half-step forward, and then paused to glance back. "What if they catch me?"

"Just tell them Murphy's handing out bee blowjobs down the hall," Ryah replied, her voice almost completely deadpan. "Pretty sure that'll be enough to make them leave you alone."

"Hehehe, beejays."

"Fuck you, Mindy."

Just as expected, Ryah and Mindy found the treasure honeycomb easily enough, and once there the pair began to reclaim their tools. While the paladin slipped back into her heavy silver armor, Ryah made a beeline for the precious scroll that still needed to be delivered back to Glory, and once she checked to make sure that the wax seals on the sides were still intact, she gave a deep sigh of relief. Before long she was tucking it into her cloak once more to nestle against a holster on her leather armor just before turning her head to see that Mindy was doubled over with her backside up, rummaging in a large wooden chest.

"What are you *doing?*" Ryah blinked, tilting her head and approaching the other woman from behind. "We've got everything they stole from us."

"Yeah but looks like they stole even more from other people!" Mindy looked up from her work, already with her hands filled with a few samples of gold jewelry. As she started to load it into the satchels hanging from her belt, she flashed the Stodar a coy smile. "So I figured...you know...why not?"

Mindy was not a particularly good paladin. Thankfully, she fit right in amidst Glory's gang.

"Yeah, guess you've got a point," Ryah murmured as she leaned forward, gazing down into the open chest. She quickly helped herself to a small handful of the jewels that were hidden within, tucking them underneath her cloak and making sure that they were neatly packed so that their rattling didn't ruin her silent movements. Afterward, she grasped a sack of gold by the tightly tied top, hefting it underneath an arm and giving a tiny grunt before shoving it towards Mindy. "Here, carry this, and I'll take the lead."

With surprising ease, the pair padded their way right back down the way they came, only to find that Marcy was already waiting for them at the end of the honeycomb hall. The dwarf was sitting squarely atop a barrel nearly as tall as her, leaning back with her legs crossed and her arms folded behind her smooth head. When she caught sight of the pair, she leaned forward, smirking and holding out her hands for the staff Mindy was carrying underneath an arm. Once she, too, was equipped for adventure again, the sturdy sorceress hopped down from the barrel and nudged it onto its side, ready to roll it straight out of the hive.

"Run into any trouble?" Ryah asked, once more taking the lead but keeping an ear out for the answer.

"Not a bit," Marcy responded and began nudging the barrel ahead to keep pace with the gang leader. "These bees *really* like fucking Murphy."

"Oh, hey, speaking of." Mindy tapped her chin thoughtfully as they neared the hive's exit. She suddenly cupped her hands around her mouth and bellowed. Any semblances of stealth and secrecy were immediately shattered as the paladin's voice roared through the hive, causing Ryah to visibly wince and facepalm. "Hey, Murphy! Are you comin' or what?!"

"I'll catch up; I'm having too much fun!" Murphy's voice echoed from deep within the hive amidst the constant wild noise of excited, horny buzzing. "I am specifically telling you to leave me behind!"

The three remaining women exchanged glances before Marcy gave a tiny grunt and started rolling the barrel forward again.

"That's the exact same thing he said last time."

***

Thus far, Ryah's group of adventurers was only half as big as it once was. Mercy was back at the island, no doubt joyfully caught between a pair of Daru, Morley was protecting their broken vessel, and Murphy was proving that in no way did he suffer from a bee allergy. Though their numbers were lessening, their loot was increasing, and to Ryah's reckoning, that still put them ahead.

Unfortunately, even though the group had already been through a shipwreck and a buzzing mugging, the most dangerous part of their trip was still ahead of them. The rocky shores north of Clover were such that the group had no hope to traverse them. The sheer cliff sides and the heavy winds would've been made for a risky trip even if they weren't trying to make the trip with a large, bulky barrel of valuable, fresh marigold honey. With the path through the cliffs inaccessible, they only had one other option: going around them.

It carried its own dangers, to be certain. They would need to swing to the west and then dip down into the Homestead, going almost an entire full circle from where they were just to get on the right path. Not only would it be an exhausting trip and add almost two days onto their travel time, it started at one of the most dangerous parts in all of Rugget: the Bile Pools. It was there at the border of the pools that the trio now stood, staring out across a sight none of them were particularly keen to ever, ever see.

The Bile Pools of Rugget were appropriately named. Nobody knew exactly how they came into being, but it was a near-marshland of toxic puddles and lakes, stretching for miles at the widest part. Clouds of hazy green fog that burned the eyes and scorched the throat were commonplace, and the pools of sludge all led to different manners of grisly death depending on their color. According to what she'd been told by Glory, Ryah knew that the blue slime burrowed right under the skin to fuse to the bone, the red ate away flesh like a rolling swarm of insects, and the green simply spontaneously combusted when it made contact with a warm-blooded creature. And as for the orange...well…

The orange could be trusted.

"Been a while since I've been here," Ryah murmured to herself. One hand nestled into her pocket to fish for a gold coin. Once she pulled it free and drew her hand away from her cloak, she slid her thumb across the surface of the coin and gazed to Mindy and Marcy nearby. "Before we do this, are you both *sure* that we don't have any other ideas? This is going to cut into our profits."

"We've got plenty," Mindy chimed up, lifting up the arm that was still carrying the heavy sack of bee-stolen gold.

"I'm sure Glory will understand if we tell her we had to spend some for a toll."

"You're not wrong, it's just…" Ryah scrunched up her nose, and the corner of her lips that wore a tiny tusk gave a twitch. "I feel like we've already made more mistakes than usual? I mean, she's already going to have to pay for a repair crew to come out for the ship, and –"

"Lass, ya always worry about her being upset, and it hasn't happened once," Marcy grunted. She swaggered forward and snatched the gold coin from Ryah's grasp. "You're her favorite. She'd sooner burn the bar's furniture than get angry at ya! Now let's get movin'!"

Before Ryah could truly respond - and even preen a little over the acknowledgement of which one of them was Glory's favorite - Marcy reared her hand back to launch the gold coin towards the edge of the Bile Pools. The trio were standing just a few feet away from one of the ponds of green slime, and even at their proximity, the fog was so dense and thick that they couldn't see where the coin would land. Indeed, they didn't even hear it fall once it vanished into the fog beyond, and for a long, lingering moment they stood in silence. Marcy walked back to the barrel and leaned against it anew, drumming her fingers on her arm before musing aloud in an impatient tone.

"So...how long do we wait?"

"Last time it only took a few minutes," Ryah murmured, moving to stand beside the dwarf. She allowed her cloak to fold around her once more, keeping her figure hidden below it and tilting her head curiously as she gazed at the fog ahead. "Just sit tight."

“Hey,” Mindy spoke up, her brow lifting and a small, playful smile tugging at her lips, “while we wait, maybe we should take a break and have ourselves som--”

“We’re not eating any of the marigold honey, Mindy,” Ryah scowled, pointing squarely at the paladin’s nose. “Last thing I need is for you two to get all horny again.”

“What trouble have we *ever* caused while we were hor--” Marcy began, only to cough and murmur when she saw Ryah’s glare. “Right, right, the shipwreck. Nevermind.”

The three women didn’t have to wait long at the edge of the Bile Pools before their ride arrived. It approached slowly at first, emerging from behind the mists like a lurking beast stalking its prey. Though it moved from the direction of the green slime pool, it neither swam nor walked, silently slithering across the surface with a rolling, oozing gait. Orange slime. It could be trusted! Or so Ryah had been told.

Thick and viscous, the ooze that approached looked like enough to fill the back of a wagon, and while they drew closer, their form began to slowly congeal and take a more definitive shape. At the very point where the orange crept over the green without disturbing it, the ooze slowly took the shape of a small rowboat’s frame, complete with two sets of wide bench seats and ample space to put luggage. While the boat portion formed, there was still orange goo taking shape, manifesting and swirling and collecting together near the very back of the impromptu boat. By the time the boat reached the edge of the slime pool - pivoting to offer an ease of boarding for the would-be passengers - the captain of this tiny, slimy ship had taken a full and complete shape.

There were no legs to speak of so much as a trunk that tethered the sticky orange body to the rest of the boat, but the longer it stretched upward, the more the figure resembled something familiar. They had shifted into a surprisingly well-sculpted set of hips and a waist with a tiny divot on both sides just before flowing into a set of arms and a full bust that resembled a human's general proportions. Sitting atop a pair of slender shoulders was an expressive and adorable head, sculpted entirely from self-animating orange slime. They emulated a surprising amount of detail, from a smooth imitation of hair that ran to their shoulders before rejoining the rest of the goo to a pair of bright, friendly eyes and plump, smiling lips. The ooze even replicated a pair of glasses set upon their face - the only manifestation of clothing they "wore." Once the ooze assumed a shape resembling a seaworthy centaur, they lifted a single hand to show that they were gripping the gold coin that Ryah had tossed. With an inquisitive tilt of their head, the ooze regarded the group with that same pleasant smile, patiently waiting for a response.

"Hello!" Ryah was completely unphased by the appearance of the ooze creature and didn't hesitate to step forward with a smile on her face and her hand fishing into her pocket for more gold coins. "We'd like to buy passage across the Bile Pools, please! Let's see. There's three of us, so would twenty gold be eno--"

"Woah, woah, woah, Ryah. We've got this." As soon as Mindy spoke up from behind, the Stodar gave a tiny grunt along with a droop of her shoulders. With a sinking feeling already in her stomach, she pivoted on a heel to see where Mindy and Marcy were standing, leaning against each other with particularly smug looks on their face. Mindy's arms were folded over her chest as she regarded the ooze from top to bottom - from the sturdy boat basin to the affable, smiling face on the humanoid portion. "How about this deal? Safe passage for the three of us through the bile pools, and in exchange, you get to fuck the two of us?"

While the ooze tilted its head and considered the offer, Ryah slapped her face and mumbled against her palm. "Why are you doing this, we have plenty of go--"

"Last time we did this, the trip was long and boring!" Marcy chimed in. "Gotta do something to keep ourselves entertained!"

Ryah simply rolled her eyes as she took a half-step back, looking to the ooze to gauge their reaction. They seemed to be considering it, narrowing their eyes through the lenses of their slimy glasses and looking both women up and down. Finally, they gazed right back up at Ryah, offered a chipper nod, and even did her the kindness of flicking that first gold coin back towards her. While the Stodar caught it and tucked it back into her pocket, she simply gave a conceding sigh and gestured for her travelling companions.

"Alright, whatever. Let's get moving." She pointed to the barrel of marigold honey, and snapped her fingers to hurry the others along. "Just try not to shake the boat too much, okay?"

Thankfully, shaking the boat wasn't a problem. Nearly a half-hour later, the ooze was slithering across the eastern edge of the bile pools and heading steadily westward, and the ride was smoother than any wagon Ryah had ever been on. Impressive, considering that the orange goo was in a constant state of flux and motion, half-sailing and half-crawling across ground and toxic puddles alike. The presence of their orange ferryslime even seemed to drive away the clouds of dense fog in their general area, ensuring that if nothing else, their trip across this dangerous region of Rugget would be safe. And for Mindy and Marcy, rather fun!

Ryah sat at the back of the boat with a small mountain of Mindy's armor and Marcy's sorcerer staff perched right beside her. She sat with her elbow on a knee and her chin in her palm, gazing with a deadpan expression towards the front of the ship where the payment for passage was being offered. She only offered the faintest sign of response when Mindy's voice was offered in her direction, riding the undertone of a long and satisfied moan that flavored her tone with a lusty heat.

"Hey, Ryah...are you *sure* you don't want to join us? Plenty of room!"

"Nah, I'm good."

Within the folds of her cloak, Ryah's fingers were wrapped around the scroll case that she was determined to deliver. She'd been secretly gripping it with a vicelike hold ever since the hive, terrified of losing it yet again and ruining her chances at returning it to Glory. The Bile Pools in particular posed a risky threat in that regard; if their form of transportation bucked in the midst of a sticky orgasm, it wasn't out of the realm of possibility that the case could go flying into some deep, dense puddle of poison. Judging by the way their day was going, Ryah wouldn't have been surprised if that happened - especially seeing as how Mindy and Marcy were doing their best to rock the boat.

The two women were completely naked at that point, which was genuinely nothing out of the ordinary for Ryah. Even as the one member of their gang that wasn't constantly distracted by lusty endeavors, the sheer number of times she'd witnessed the dwarf and the paladin without their clothes by incidental glances had to be over a hundred. This wasn't even the first time she sat by and watched them have sex with someone. Hell, it wasn't even the first time she'd watched them do it for the expressed purpose of paying for passage!

"I think we all need to have a discussion about staying focused on the job when we get back to Glory's bar."

Ryah's voice went completely ignored to the point she doubted the other two even heard her - and in truth, she couldn't blame them. Mindy and Marcy were both half-engulfed in orange goo as the ferryslime enjoyed their payment, their humanoid form having expanded to entwine around the pair and slither forward with constantly shifting, wiggling tentacles of thick, citrus-colored ooze. At that current moment, Mindy was filling the air with the sounds of her desperate moans as the ooze was steadily pumping two separate tendrils into her lower entrances, while Marcy was so lost in the slime that the only thing Ryah could see was the look of her ecstatic, orgasmic face.

Through it all, their host for the trip looked completely serene as they shifted about the ship, sinking into themself and reemerging like a prairie dog popping up and down from the ground. In one moment, they were behind Mindy, moving their hands around the human's body to fondle at her lovely, full bust, and the next, they were looming above Marcy, one hand resting atop the dwarf's bald head as they bucked their hips forward to feed the dwarf an impressive length dangling from their lap. At one point, the slime sunk down only to appear again sitting beside Ryah, popping up from below Mindy's armor and filling it out perfectly as they flopped into a sitting position. Once there, the armored ooze mimicked Ryah's sitting position perfectly, and even nudged the Stodar with a friendly smile on their face.

"Hmm?" She blinked, arching a brow as she regarded the other. "No, sorry. I don't want to be rude; I'm just not interested."

The slime wordlessly smiled, and Ryah watched as the floor of the boat shifted slightly - only for a sudden, short table to spring up from the bottom. It came fully equipped with the imitation of a chess set, every piece the same orange tint as the creature they were riding and ready to play. Ryah tilted her head curiously, looking from the set to the face of the smiling slime that was wearing Mindy's armor.

"Play? Sure, we could, but what abou--" Ryah cut herself off as she looked to the other end of the boat only to see that Mindy and Marcy not only were still having fun, but they were *each* joined by duplicates of the slime's humanoid upper half. They both looked identical to the first from the smooth hair down to the shoulders to the cute face, and each even included a pair of fake eyeglasses perched upon their faces. One of them was burying said face between Mindy's thighs while the paladin convulsed in pleasure and the other had positioned themselves directly facing Marcy, thrusting a set of orange tentacles into the dwarf's entrances with surprising vigor and power. Neither Ryah's travelling companions or the other two parts of the slime seemed to even acknowledge the Stodar's presence, and Ryah simply shrugged and turned back to the ooze with a smile.

"Okay, sure. Let's play," she agreed and let a single hand escape from the folds of her cloak. "I'll go first."

***

Twelve hours later, Ryah was sitting on a stump in the heart of the Homestead. She had finally put the Bile Pools behind her and made headway along the path, and it was her deep, *deep* hope that by the time the next morning came, she'd be able to return the scroll case to Glory and receive her well-deserved reward. The Homestead was relatively safe for a seasoned adventurer like herself, and that was a particularly good thing considering that her party was one smaller. Marcy was having so much fun with the orange ferryslime that she decided to stay behind, presumably to enjoy a few more round trips around the Bile Pools. It left Ryah alone with the paladin Mindy, who had taken on the responsibility of rolling the barrel of marigold honey along the road until they finally made camp.

And it was here at that camp, with a fire slowly burning and the two women settling in for the evening, that Ryah gave Mindy a sharp gaze as she gestured from side to side. "You take the first watch," she ordered just as she slid from the stump to sit on the ground, resting her back against it. This close to the fire, she was nice and cozy, and after everything they'd been through so far, a nice, warm nap sounded like just the thing to take the edge of. "The Homestead's not that dangerous, but you never know when we might run into bandits or an errant gnoll from the Feral Hills."

"You've got it!" Mindy nodded from her own position, kneeling on the grass and stripped down once more to her bra and panties. This time she had a good reason; she was fiercely scrubbing at the inside of her breastplate, grumbling lightly to herself while she did so. "Can't believe you let that ooze wear my armor. Everything's sticky!"

"Mindy, at one point, I swear there was more of them inside of you than there was outside, so I don't want to hear it." Ryah rolled her eyes and huffed as she folded her arms across her chest. "I'm gonna get some sleep."

"Hey, are you sure you wanna doze off already?" Mindy pressed, looking up from her work and tilting her head. She nudged the nearby barrel with her elbow and wiggled her brow towards the Stodar. "Y'know, now that it's just the two of us, maybe we could crack this baby open and help ourse--"

"Goodnight, Mindy," Ryah grumbled, and didn't even bother to open her eyes before she followed that statement with a chaser. "Oh, and do *not* eat any of that honey!"

It wasn't long after that Ryah finally managed to fall asleep, fatigued from a long day that felt like it would never end. She did so confident that she'd made her orders clear: Mindy was to stand guard, protect their camp, and under no circumstances was she to sample the marigold honey that would repay Glory for the damage to her ship. Given that Ryah was crystal clear about everything and that they were already at the end of a very long and stressful day, she really knew she had no right to be surprised when she woke up to the sounds of wild, vigorous sex.

"For fuck's sakes, Mindy."

Hours later, after heading south from the edge of the Bile Pools and into the farmland of the Homestead, the remaining pair of adventurers set up camp that Ryah *hoped* would mark the last delay before returning to Glory's Hole.

And now, having just woken from a traveler's nap, Ryah was left wiping the sleep from her eyes, gazing towards a campfire that had diminished into embers. The light of the stars and moon above were still enough for the sharp-eyed Stodar to see the source of the noise that woke her, and with an irate grunt, Ryah regarded her final travelling companion and someone she was *sure* she hadn't met before - a massive, towering minotaur.

Both naked. Both sweaty. Both with honey glaze spread across their bodies.

For the moment, Ryah just sat with a deadpan expression on her face, watching the two go at it. She could only assume the minotaur had wandered down from the Feral Hills looking to hunt game in the Homestead, but he seemed plenty happy with what he'd discovered. A hulking, bipedal beast, he sported thick brown fur across his entire body and sported a bovine head with horns that stretched even longer than his already-broad shoulders. At that moment, he was kneeling in the grass with his hands locked around Mindy's waist, who was bent on her hands and knees in front of him. While the paladin unleashed a stream of depraved and aroused moans, the minotaur's noises resembled those one might find in a barn - a little strange considering they were an intelligent species, but the reasoning soon became clear as Mindy groaned with delight.

"M-Moo for me, you big fucking stud!" The paladin's fingers dug into the dirt, her knees spread and her backside constantly slapping against the lap of the towering brute. "Moo if you're digging this holy pussy!"

Mindy was not a particularly good paladin, but her new lover didn't seem to mind. The minotaur surged forward with strength and ferocity, his massive figure slamming ahead again and again while the paladin was left bouncing in the grass below them. Each thrust came with a loud grunt and the more subtle sound of his length dipping deep, gripped fiercely by nethers that were particularly wet thanks to the marigold honey's notorious effects. The beast nearly roared as his head tilted back, maw opening as he began to obey the command of this *very* friendly paladin.

"Moooo mooooooo-woah, fuck, your friend's awake!"

"Ryah, hi!" Mindy blinked, looking towards Ryah through a few locks of dangling, curly black hair that were matted against her face. "I'd like you to meet my new friend! His name is...uh…"

Ryah just stared with a deadpan expression, waiting for Mindy to come up with something.

"His name, his name, it's...it's…" Mindy bit her bottom lip, nibbling it briefly before continuing.
"Horace...Bullcock?"

"That's actually really close," Horace murmured and didn't stop thrusting.

Ryah just gave a disappointed sigh at the pair and pushed her hands to her knees to start standing up. She jerked herself up to her feet and allowed her cloak to fold around her once more, sneaking a hand within to make sure the sealed scroll case was still perfectly in place. Once she did, Ryah casually walked over to where the barrel of marigold honey had clearly been opened, and when she peered inside, her fears were concerned. Half of it was gone, and what was left looked like it was sporting a *lot* more minotaur fur than Glory would've been happy with.

"I'll see you back at the bar, Mindy," Ryah simply sighed, held back the urge to give a long and tired yawn, and turned on a heel to start walking down the starlit path. She'd make better time on her own anyway. "It was nice meeting you, Horace."

***

By the time Ryah crossed the Clover city limits, she was exhausted. It had been a long, tiring road to return home, but even if she was dragging her feet across the finish line, it was still nice to be back. Clover was a place of bustling activity no matter the hour, and even though Ryah's march from the Homestead to simply home had taken her almost an entire day, she made the trip without incident. Funny, that. Almost like the rest of her gang held a certain level of responsibility with how things typically went.

Regardless, Ryah made her way along the path to Glory's Hole, and the closer she got, the more spring she found in her step. By the time she caught sight of that welcoming building in nearly the dead center of Clover, she was practically sprinting, weaving in between the crowds and circumventing the line that was forming at the entrance. The tantalizing smells of freshly cooked tavern food and the sounds of joyous revelry were hanging high in the air, and before she'd even touched the door, Ryah was starting to feel invigorated. After a small but friendly nod to the Daru woman serving as a bouncer, Ryah made her way across the threshold and finally returned back home.

And as soon as she had a single foot past the door, she was noticed and greeted with welcoming arms.

"Ryah, lass!" the familiar sound of the bar's owner filled the air, and Ryah's eyes darted to the counter to see Glory beaming back at her. She was already handing off a set of drinks to one of the waitstaff as she darted from behind the bar to approach, beaming from ear to ear and wearing the same loving, friendly look that seemed to almost plaster her amicable features. When the owner of the bar moved, even the most inebriated patrons knew to step out of the way, and as they parted a path to the Stodar at the door, Glory followed along it to her destination. Once there, with a pair of surprisingly strong and sturdy arms, the dwarf snatched the slender Stodar in a hug, picking her a few inches up off the floor with ease. "I was starting to worry about ya!"

"Hi, Glory. It's nice to be home," Ryah squeaked when she was first picked up and squeezed but didn't hesitate to return the embrace. While she threaded her arms around the dwarf's shoulders and bent slightly down to give her a proper hug, the Stodar's eyes drifted briefly closed, holding her in a familiar embrace. "I'm sorry it took so long, you just...you wouldn't believe how things fell apart this time."

"Oh yeah?" Glory asked, leaning back on a heel and clapping her only returning agent on the back. She began leading Ryah back through the bar, following the same parted path, and towards an empty spot at the counter. "The Daru didn't give you any problems, did they? I sent Mercy along with you knowing that she'd likely help smooth things over."

"Uh...you were right about that one," Ryah murmured, rubbing the back of her head and giving a sheepish chuckle. As she swung onto a stool and slipped a hand into her cloak, her fingers wrapped around the sealed scroll case once more. "The last I saw of Mercy, she was wedged between two of them. And I'm pretty sure there were four more waiting their turn."

"Ha! Sounds about right," Glory had turned her back at that point, having snatched up a tall mug and a few different bottles. She was already in the process of making up a fresh drink for the returning adventurer, and Ryah leaned forward to steal a glance at the components. No spirits, all sweetener. *Just* the way she liked it. "I'm sure she'll catch up. What about the others?"

"Well…" Ryah rolled her shoulders as she put the case on the counter, though she still held her hand atop it for safekeeping. She wasn't about to let go of it now, this close to the finish line! "Murphy stayed behind with the beefolk. And Marcy is with that ferryslime we met a few months ago. Mindy made a new friend out in the Homestead, and...oh! I'm sorry, Glory, we wrecked the ship on the north coast. Morley stayed behind to keep an eye on it."

"Did he, now?" Glory arched a brow as she spun around, putting the mug squarely in front of Ryah. "I'm sure the circumstances of your crash and his decision to stay behind had nothing to do with the fact that he's been dating a merfolk from up that way."

One of Ryah's eyes gently twitched, and her fingers briefly tightened upon the scroll case before she pushed it towards the edge of the counter.

"Could you take this off my hands, please?" the Stodar managed to squeak out politely, and as soon as Glory did so, she swept her hands to the offered mug. With her irritation rising high and her desire to smack Morley silly shooting up along with it, the adventurer took a quick, long drink, and almost immediately calmed. Pure sweetness assaulted her senses thanks to a non-alcoholic but incredibly fruity drink, and when she dragged her tongue across her lips she made a sound of tiny, true satisfaction. "Thank you."

"Thank *you,* lass!" Glory beamed as she popped open the scroll case, upended the parchment within, and gave a big, hearty laugh. Once she confirmed what it was, she tucked the case against her belt, flashing a smile to the

Stodar once more. "I'll get this to Letty tonight, see what she can make of it. Even if we have to repurpose some of the brewery to make use of the Daru brewing techniques, it'll be worth it. Maybe *this* will finally be the nail in Corelune's Cafe's coffin!"

"I hope so, Glory," Ryah responded, though admittedly, she had heard those exact words many, many times before. Not that she minded; it was all a part of the sounds of home. "I really hope so."

Ryah remained in the bar for a little longer - mostly until Glory dipped down into the basement levels of her bar to deliver the scroll. Before she did, she promised that Ryah's reward would be waiting for her in her quarters, a tiny room near the very top floor of the tavern. Past a separate set of guards that welcomed Ryah with a smile, the Stodar made her way past the points of Glory's Hole that most travellers in Clover ever saw and into the area that was strictly, explicitly for employees only. When she slipped past the door leading to her quarters, the adventurer was in dire, dire need of a rest, and it was there she found it.

Along with a reward that was well-earned and even more well-appreciated.

Front and center in her room, a special dining table had been set up with a single chair and an array of food freshly made while she'd been waiting at the bar. Steamed vegetables from the Homestead's finest stock with heavy dollops of butter still melting amidst them, an entire loaf of bread so fresh from the oven that she could see the heat, a bowl of hot chicken soup larger than her head, and most scrumptious of all, half the table filled with the finest desserts Glory's Hole had to offer.

Ryah stepped up to the table with a smile, only to then notice that the chair was already occupied. Thankfully, not by someone so much as some*thing* - a large burlap sap neatly tied at the top with a small note attached. Idly Ryah slid a finger underneath the note and glanced at it, reading aloud with a smile. "Another job well done, lass. Always nice to see you come home."

Ryah smiled softly as her fingers hooked against the handle of the bag and lifted it, moving it straight to the ground. Judging by the weight and the jingling sounds it made, she could only assume it was a heaping sack of gold - just like every time she dragged her feet across the door, exhausted and deserving of a reward. From there, Ryah settled into her seat and gazed at the offering of food before her, her hands dropping to the table as she allowed herself to sit and savor the moment. The smells. The sights. The sheer warmth of being back in her quarters and knowing that anything she wanted - whether it was a tasty meal or a motherly hug from the dwarf that employed her - was well within her grasp.

Elsewhere in Rugget, Daru women were no doubt taking turns trying to split Mercy in two. Morley was likely kneeling at the edge of the sea and spending time with his merfolk girlfriend. Murphy was probably regretting some very impulsive and very sticky decisions, while Marcy was thankful that she didn't have any hair she had to scrub orange slime out of. And Mindy - if the last time Ryah spotted her was any indication - was taking the bull by the horns…and alo various other parts.

Ryah was happy to let them have their fun. Hers came in the unmistakably wonderful feeling she had every time she returned home.

And a massive sack of gold she had absolutely no intention of sharing with them.

As she finishes, you're already on your second piece of apple pie - which Glory seems to have decided is not, in fact, good enough for Ryah. As the free food and drink continue to flow, the dwarf looks downright wistful with thoughts of her cherished friend slash employee slash surrogate daughter, and it's easy to see why. Judging from the story, Ryah had a focus that a lot of others lacked, and that served her well in the relentlessly horny region of Rugget. When you observe to Glory that it must be difficult finding staff that doesn't get distracted by a bit of exposed flesh, the dwarf roars with laughter, nodding vigorously in response.

"Oh, you don't know the half of it," she chuckles. "It can be a real hassle keeping the kegs filled and the larder stocked sometimes. But Ryah's never failed to come through for me, which is why my girl deserves a feast every time she walks through that door. A celebration every time she comes home. A place that's warm, inviting, and cozy every time she gets inside Glory's Hole."

You blink again. Seriously, how does she not realize how this sounds?

Monsters and Their Hunger

It'd be hard for anyone to argue that Glory's Hole isn't a wild place. You're not sure if it's like this every night, but you're four hours in to your first visit, and things have been lively seen you stepped through the door. The event of the hour takes place near the front door where that towering brute of a Daru woman works, keeping out the troublemakers while inviting the welcome company in with a broad smile.

She looks damn near like a goddess, towering a solid few feet over even the tallest in the tavern, with long curls of dark hair that travel past the boundary of broad, buff shoulders. Like most of the Daru, she looks like she's made of muscle first and foremost with everything else added for excitement, including large breasts tightly-confined within a shirt struggling bravely to keep her in check and a pair of snug leather pants that could just as easily be painted on.

You're not the only one whose eyes have been caught by her, and it doesn't even take fascination with her size and presence to keep glancing over. Every half hour or so, someone's tried something - from the thief you yourself foiled to the random patron trying to sneak out on their tab. Most of the time, she's stopped every last problem with minimal issue thanks to a sharp glare and a looming shadow, and every time, the crowd goes silent as if hoping that this time - this time - they'd get to see her in action.

The time comes in the midst of the fourth hour, when she grabs a scrawny elf man by the scruff of his shirt collar, easily lifting him up a few feet in the air. As he flails and fidgets, the bouncer walks him straight over to the bar, and while Glory's moved on to tend to other patrons, you can clearly overhear the discussion that takes place.

"Caught him pouring a drink into this," the bouncer growls and tosses the dwarf a closed flask with an underhand pitch. Glory catches it in a smooth motion and uncorks the top, and the otherwise-affable hostess takes a sharp sniff of the drink. Her expression immediately sours.

"My Elfelpin Brandy," Glory practically growls, just before taking a few swigs straight from the flask and licking her lips clean of the flavor. "Corelun send you in here? Trying to get a sample of my special blend?"

"N-No, no, I promise!" The elf looks panicked - as anyone would be dangling from the powerful fist of a glorious, grand Daru woman. "I swear, she didn't--I mean, I don't---who's Corelun? I never heard of he--"

Glory cuts him off by gesturing to the door, and the Daru simply nods as she begins carrying him in that direction. While the bouncer escorts the spirit spy from the premises, the dwarf herself finds her eyes upon you again, chuckling as she wiggles the flask from side to side.

"One of the few drinks I let outside the premises," she explains, and slides it across the counter to sit before you. "My local rival's always trying to get her filthy hands on it. Nice to have a Daru on hand to take care of problems like that."

You don't ask, but that doesn't matter - Glory's already lifting herself up to the stool across the counter, smirking as she looks in the direction of where her bouncer went. As the sound of the elf unceremoniously getting ejected fills the air, Glory's grin grows, and you can already tell...she's about to do it again.

"Y'know, if there's one thing I've learned, it's how important it is to have a Daru on your side." She gives a small wave and an approving nod to her bouncer, who immediately resumes her post. "They're as tough as they come. And from my experience, even when you meet one of 'em that seems so bullheaded there's no getting through to her, well...sometimes? They'll surprise ya with how that big, tough facade fades away."

The farther north that one travelled across the lands of Rugget, the tighter survival was tied to rage. There was a long road snaking its way across the countryside most often taken by those making deliveries to the elven town of Glint, and along that path, travelers faced perils from the Feral Hills in the west and the Bile Pools in the east - two of the most notoriously dangerous regions in all of Rugget. Everyone knew that, from the simple farmers in Homestead to the cutthroat brigands at Port Failure. What was *less* commonly known, however, was that if a travelling party made their way to the walls of Glint and then kept heading even further north, things only got worse.

Nestled in the rocky valleys north of Glint, the goblins were deeply entrenched. Safe and secure, from their caves and shelters they plotted violent assaults on everyone from random travelers to the walls of the elven city itself. Vicious, vindictive, angry little creatures, they were little more than bundles of cream-colored muscle holding makeshift daggers and clubs, and their raiding parties were one of the primary reasons travelling that far north was akin to a death sentence. They were the devious threat of the wilds, ones that would sneak up and tear someone asunder while they were distracted by the gnolls and the undead and the iron boars.

And that night, deep in one of the valleys flanked on both sides by lines of goblin caves, those wicked little monsters were in a state of panic. Their raiding camp was considered a fortress of violence, so well-defended by sharp-toothed warriors that it couldn't possibly be broken. At least not until it met a warrior of sufficient skill, power, and rage. Lyeth had plenty of all three.

"Yraaaaaugh!" The roar that crossed over the countryside was enough to send animals scurrying up trees in fear, a furious bellow that spoke of a threat that could not be contained by the conventional dangers of Rugget. Sure enough, riding over the horizon on the heels of that thundering bellow came the frantic screeches of terrified goblins - shrill and wild and not weighed down by a single ounce of courage. Understandably so, considering the monster that now raged throughout their camp. "Hraaaaaa!"

She was glorious in her fury, a woman of almost unspeakable ferocity in the field of combat.

The Daru were a well-known race of amazons from the islands and mountains past the Rugget border, a loosely knit collection of some of the most skilled warriors the mainland would ever know. They were renowned for their towering heights and impressively muscular builds, the smallest of them reaching seven feet and three hundred pounds of solid, toned muscle. To Lyeth, such a Daru would be considered a runt, just as the frantically panicking goblins were little more than vermin scurrying desperately away from her. At nearly nine feet tall and sporting curls of thick blonde hair as long as the average goblin's height, this particular Daru moved through their ranks without flinching from their blows and without the slightest acknowledgement of their yelps for mercy. After all, if the sight of nearby wagons and freshly picked human bones were any indication, it was not something they themselves were akin to extending.

"More! More of you! I'll drive every last one of you into the dirt!" Lyeth's voice bellowed through the camp, and her muscles went taut as she spotted a new squad of goblins rushing to the defense of the others. They were heavily armored in patchwork metal and mostly carrying makeshift weapons - spears with rusty heads and crude clubs with shreds of metal pounded into the face. It was all too clear that these little monsters had been relying on sheer numbers and reputation to keep their base of operations safe, but now...now everything was crumbling underneath the weight of primal Daru fury.

"Ohh, you really think that'll stop me?!" Like a charging bull, Lyeth rushed ahead with little regard for her own safety. Her impressively sculpted body was only barely covered with thick straps of deep brown leather and hide, from a keenly positioned strip that held her hefty breasts against her chest to those that crossed down her forearms and over her wrists and palms, leaving her knuckles brandishing metal studs across them. Those strips of leather were all that she needed for offense and defense alike, and the opponents she stood against didn't have a chance.

As Lyeth met the gang of armored goblins she immediately sent them scattering with a heavy kick to the center of the mob, forcing their unit to scatter while the goblin that took the kick launched up into the air. Seamlessly, Lyeth snatched the little creature in mid-air with one powerful hand that had no trouble seizing him by the chest, at which point the Daru woman gave a thundering, triumphant laugh.

"Let me help you escape!" She beamed, reared back with the hand holding the flailing goblin, and launched him over the horizon. For dozens and dozens of feet, the wailing creature soared from the valley, emitting a frantic scream as it did so. The warrior didn't wait to hear the subsequent thud, however, turning on a heel and gazing at the rest of the horde that were coming for her with every weapon they could scavenge from their nests. As one of them charged her with a rusty spear only to be met with a helmet-shattering punch from the iron-studded fist of the Daru, Lyeth gazed over her shoulder and offered out a much friendlier cry, complete with a broad smile and flashing, violent eyes. "Audrey, this was a great idea! Aren't you having fun?!"

At the very sidelines of the conflict there was another woman, neither goblin nor Daru, standing motionless and watching the battle take place. She was a strange one seemingly human but with skin as pale as freshly squeezed milk framed by smooth, straight hair as black as pitch. Her face was an expressionless mask with her eyes half-open to stare unblinkingly ahead and lips drawn thin. Her shoulders sagged, and her arms hung limp at her sides, back slightly hunched, and her entire body was wrapped within the confines of a loose-fitting robe of black and purple silks. The robe itself travelled so far down that not even her feet could be seen, keeping her almost completely shrouded. Even when Lyeth called to her, she didn't make any conscious response, simply staring ahead at the battlefield while the goblins continued an increasingly futile assault.

Her lack of reaction didn't seem to bother the Daru, who simply cackled in manic delight as her rampage continued. A particularly bold goblin managed to jump high enough to bring his dagger to bear across her body, though the blade made little more than a scratch across her smooth flesh even with every ounce of his strength behind the strike. Lyeth merely paused, smirked at the goblin that was rapidly questioning his life choices, and then reached down to grab him by the scruff of his collar.

"Let me show you how to wield a weapon." The blonde beamed before suddenly spinning on a heel and using the screaming thing like a club against its kin. The sound of armor bending and breaking filled the air along with the noise of cracking bones and chattering teeth, all riding along a constant current of terrified, frantic screams from panicked little beasts. While Lyeth continued her rampage through the camp the goblin numbers continued to surge, and all the while, Audrey remained on the sidelines. Arms limp, shoulders sagged, eyes lidded.

Lidded, but locked on Lyeth. Always.

***

"Goodness! This...this was more than we ever could have hoped for!" The sound of grateful farmers wasn't anywhere near as satisfying as that of shrieking goblins, at least to Lyeth's reckoning. Still, she stood there, towering over the people of a small village about a half hour after their battle finished, keeping her fists clenched and her tongue behind her teeth while they praised her. The elder of the village - a particularly weathered looking man sporting a crutch and an eyepatch - was taking the lead in pouring adoration over the visiting pair. "Our scouts saw it all take place! You...you completely routed them! They won't be raiding our homes or killing our livestock anymore!"

"You two are heroes!" An appreciative-looking young woman practically danced before the pair, folding her hands together in a pleading fashion and gazing up at Lyeth. And, to a lesser extent, the unsettlingly pale looking woman in the robe that seemed as attached to the Daru as her shadow. "I sure hope you'll stay for our celebration tonight in your honor! Why...maybe you and I could...maybe…"

"Our reward," Lyeth simply demanded and stuck out her massive, upturned hand. "Now."

Some adventurers were happy to waste their time having 'fun' with the farmers they helped. Lyeth and Audrey were more...goal-oriented.

The farmers of the tiny settlement blinked in surprise at just how forward Lyeth was but considering her size and the deeds she'd already accomplished, none of them seemed bold enough to betray the terms of their deal. Mere moments after the pair reported their success at the goblin raiding camp, they were headed right back there for the evening;

after all, the hour was getting late, and it had been recently vacated. While they walked, Lyeth held open the sack of silvers they'd been rewarded with, scowling fiercely as she stuck a hand into the bag and flipped the coins around in the search for anything resembling gold.

"Pathetic," the Daru woman grunted and stuffed the sack into a leather pouch hanging at her hips. She was taking the lead between the two but, as always, Audrey was close at hand, drifting mere steps behind her and moving with a surprising grace. Not only were the pale-skinned woman's feet not visible, but the movement of her legs couldn't be seen through the fabric of her robe, the strange young woman practically gliding at the heels of her companion. Her fairly irritable, frustrated companion. "I can't believe we have to work this far north. The jobs are harder, and the pay is worse." She huffed and quickly glanced over her shoulder to glare at the woman close at hand. "This is all your fault, you know. Cross wouldn't have cared in the slightest about what we did if we slapped a pile of Stodar Warmaster gold on her table. We'd be *living* at Port Failure."

Audrey didn't respond. She didn't even tilt her head to look up at the woman towering above her and simply continued her slow and smooth pace forward. Not that Lyeth was particularly surprised at that, and soon the Daru growled as she gazed forward again and took a wide, angry kick at a nearby dented goblin helmet. They must've been nearing the abandoned camp - either that, or she managed to get *much* better distance on some of the ones she threw.

"I don't care *what* the runt's little cat friend told you," Lyeth grumbled and tucked her hands against the thick leather strap that served as her makeshift belt. She slid her thumbs between the material and her waistline, the rest of her powerful fingers draped casually across the sides though still tightened around the entire belt when she hit a particularly sharp tinge of frustration or anger. "We could've delivered them and taken our gold. And if that Stodar bitch tried anything, well...we could've fuckin' taken her, too! I mean...look at this!"

As she spoke, the pair finally arrived back at the site of their conquest, the thoroughly demolished goblin camp. Dozens, maybe even *hundreds* of the little raiders had either been trampled by Lyeth or sent screaming to the very outer edges of Rugget and all because of the two of them. Really more Lyeth than Audrey, but it wasn't like the Daru to be selfish with the credit.

"We did this in a single afternoon, Audrey," Lyeth's eyes passed over the proof of their destructive power with an almost wistful look in her eyes, her heavy chest drawing in and falling once more at the behest of a deep sigh. Her hands squeezed tightly at her belt as she bit back a little of her fury, voice softening as she let the thought sink in. "We're the most dangerous women in Rugget. Hell, maybe even in all of Sombfal! Why should we be out here scavenging for jobs?"

The quiet, almost contemplative moment led Lyeth to a revelation, and her brow lifted just as her smile began to grow. One of her hands pulled forward, and she snapped her fingers in growing pride over her idea. She flashed Audrey's deadpan expression a broad and shameless smile before she spoke. "Hey, hey, here's what we'll do…"

When Lyeth began, Audrey did something dramatic. She tilted her head two inches to the side and allowed her eyes to shift towards the Daru. It was dramatic *for her,* at least.

With the dark eyes of the emotionless woman resting upon her Lyeth practically bubbled over with excitement, rocking back and forth on her heels as she gestured to the carnage before them. “See all this? See this big fuckin’ wreck of things? What if we go down to Port Failure and do the same to *them?!*”

It was a bold statement, even for the impulsive Daru that so often acted on instinct and fury. Putting aside the fact that Port Failure was literal weeks’ worth of travel to the south from where they were, it was quite possibly the most fortified place in Rugget. Not even the Clover bankhouse could boast the same sort of defenses that Port Failure did - that of a small army of cutthroats, mercenaries, pirates, and legitimate adventurers that all paid fealty to their leader. To Lyeth, it made perfect sense! Kick down the door, punt the bouncer into the ceiling, and give Cross an ultimatum: start calling her and Audrey the new queens in town or see what kind of distance she could make from the shoreline with a running start. There was truly boundless confidence in Lyeth’s voice as she floated the idea, the sort of shameless, headstrong determination that had kept her alive for this long in dangerous lands.

Despite how assured she was, however, Audrey didn’t seem quite so keen on the idea. She simply stood. And stared.

“Well? Great idea, isn’t it? Just think about the look on that old hag’s face when all her little pets bow down to us!”

Audrey simply continued to stare, unblinking and unflinching, completely silent.

“Ohh and think about all the treasure she’s got stored up somewhere!” Lyeth seemed undaunted, pushing past Audrey’s resistance with a large and sinister grin. “Do you think we should keep Cross behind bars, so she has to watch us enjoy her loot? No, no, what am I saying? She's way too crafty. We'll throw her ass off the lighthouse as soon as we get our hands on her, just to make sure she doesn't escape. So? Should we get going?"

The question was left hanging in the air, directed towards a woman that wasn't known for voicing her opinion. Still, Audrey let the question sit between them as she returned her gaze back towards the goblin wreckage before them. There she stood, arms limp and shoulders sagging, just before she began to move once more. Not in the direction that would set them on the road towards Port Failure but deeper into the goblin raiding camp, abandoned and private as it was.

"Audrey, I think you're--h-hey!" It took Lyeth a few seconds before she wrapped her head around the choice that had been made, at which point she stumbled behind the robed woman in a reversal of their typical marching order. "That's a no? You're not even going to think about it?" Once more, frustration flared within the mighty Daru, her cheeks growing red her fists tightening, and one mighty foot crashing down onto the dirt with an almost childlike stomp. "Seriously, Audrey?! You want to just stay here?! What in the name of all of fucking Sombfal are we going to do up here in the middle of nowhere without a single gold to our names?!"

At that question, Audrey stopped and slowly started to turn. Just like how she walked, her pivot was downright unnatural without a single movement to her legs visible beneath the fabric of her robe. Like a flat-based doll simply twisted on a tabletop, the porcelain-skinned woman faced

Lyeth and stared. This time, however, she actually gave her companion a proper response.

The fingers of her typically limp hands stretched out, grabbed at the fabric of her robe, and pulled it forward just a few short inches. It wasn't much, and what was visible underneath was a sight that very, very few individuals on Sombfal had ever bore witness to, but it changed Lyeth's tune with surprising speed and efficiency.

"Okay, yes, I *would* rather we do that, instead."

Lyeth was a brute, but she was far from unreasonable.

***

The path to that moment had been long and frustrating for Lyeth. The argument could be certainly made that it was all because of her own actions; after all, it was she that decided to betray the trust of the loosely knit Homestead adventurer's guild, and it was she that opted to side with a Stodar Warmaster against the personal favorite of the guild's mistress. She had lost more fights than won over the past few months, or at the very least, lost the ones that mattered the most. She was a durable woman with the constant companionship of a trusted ally, but not even her incredible strength and imposing physique could protect her from the shame of failure. With the Homestead having rejected them, with her own native home as distant as the sun, there was little place left in Sombfal for Lyeth...aside, of course, for right beside Audrey.

The Daru woman was stretched back at that point, resting in one of the more comfortable caves that the pair found in the goblin encampment. Lyeth's sheer girth made it a tricky feat to find a spot that accommodated her, and in truth, she couldn't fully stand up within it. Not that it mattered; she doubted she'd be properly upright until well into the morning again. For the moment, her back was pressed flush against the cave wall while she sat with knees bent and feet firmly planted on the ground, thighs idly spread in a manner that was downright seductive. Seductive, at least, for someone that was accustomed to the field of battle than anything resembling romance.

"This is what you want, hmm?" the towering woman practically purred from her spot in the back of the cave, eyes darting to the figure standing in its entrance. She smoothed her hands across her body in slow and alluring fashion, moving over the well-sculpted and defined muscles of her abdomen and her full breasts all the way up into the locks of long, curly blonde hair. The longer she teased her powerful fingers across herself, the more the Daru found herself smirking, eyes flashing with a particular delight as her heart began to race quicker. Moments such as this didn't befall her often, but when they did...they were worth relishing. "And here I thought that night a few months ago was a one-time thing. Guess you needed some time to recover?"

Audrey stood in the mouth of the cave, watching Lyeth with an expressionless gaze and predictably saying nothing. Her arms hung as flaccid as the bangs that framed the sides of her head, and she didn't even blink as the wind whipped around the entrance and across her comparatively smaller figure. She responded to Lyeth with neither a look nor a single word, but that didn't mean the Daru's question went unanswered. Far from it, as the bottom edge of Audrey's robe was slowly starting to shift and ripple with movement from within.

“Mmm...don’t think I’ve ever seen you this worked up before.” Lyeth chuckled, and slowly dragged her tongue across her lips from corner to corner just before biting down against the bottom one. She held it firmly in place as she drew in a long and hungry breath, hands lowering to the rocky floor below and fingers digging against the ground. She was bracing herself, either in preparation for what was about to come for her or to simply stop herself from pouncing on the pale-skinned, strange young woman standing nearly a dozen feet away. After all, she made for such an irresistible target! “How long have you been wanting this? Watching me fight...all those long nights on the road...I bet I had you so hot you were ready to burst.”

It was no question that the vast majority of people would look at the strangeness that was Audrey and not even notice the subtle shifting of her robe. They’d simply focus on the woman’s expressionless face and the way her entire posture was that of a broken doll on a hook, completely ignorant to what lurked beneath the thick black and purple cloth draped across her body. And while Lyeth was far from what one could call insightful, when it came to Audrey? She was the only one with her eyes fully open. And for being that precious single person in all of Sombfal, she was generously rewarded in shameless, indulgent pleasure.

Audrey was slow to take action, but when she did it was fast and wild - and absolutely, overwhelmingly undeniable. That gentle shifting of her robe was the brief tinge of static on the air before a thunderstorm, though instead of the crack of lightning and a torrent of rain, Lyeth was assaulted by a sudden flurry of motion from just underneath the other woman’s robe. As the cloth lifted, Lyeth was just able to give a tiny gasp before they rushed towards her, laughing in a state of wild pleasure before she found herself fully engulfed.

"Yes, yes! Give me all of you!"

Tentacles. There were dozens of them in that moment, ranging in width and length as they darted forward like the lashes of whips. Some of them were smooth and rubbery over their entire surface while others sported suckers on one side, which connected to Lyeth's flesh as they wrapped around the bare parts of her calves and thighs. The majority of the tentacles were the same pitch black as Audrey's hair while others were a soothing, dark purple, the colors appearing across all varieties of lengths and strengths as they launched against Lyeth.

In just a few short seconds, Lyeth went from laying back and teasing her companion with idle fingers across her breasts to swarmed by an endless sea of appendages, each one writhing across her, squeezing her impressive physique, studying her curves with every teasing, twitching tip. Lyeth herself had difficulty moving within the swarm, but her impressive Daru strength allowed it with a bit of effort, just so she could pull a particularly thick tentacle to caress her cheek, tilting her head to offer it a tiny, chaste kiss. Or at least, as chaste as their interactions got.

"More of them than last time," the Daru mused, glancing down not only at the swarm that had overtaken her, but from wall to wall within the cave. There wasn't much stonework to be seen anymore, replaced now by the slithering, twitching movements of Audrey's expansion network of appendages. She couldn't even see past the smaller woman to the rest of the camp outside the cave, since when they all suddenly emerged, Audrey's limp-hanging body had tilted forward. Now the broken doll hung there at an angle, lifted entirely by her tentacles which fanned behind her like the feathers of a twisted peacock. She was still completely expressionless, and her arms still hung flaccid at her sides, but her eyes had at least trained upon Lyeth. The two women met each other's gaze, and the Daru made sure to hold that contact as she tightened her hands against the rubbery embrace squeezing her from every angle, her voice dropping low, lusty, and intense. "So...are you going to fuck me with them, or did you just want a little hug?"

The smug smirk that spread across Lyeth's face combined with her playfully taunting words were enough to force the tentacles into action. She groaned as she felt nearly every muscle in her body constricted by coils of powerful, smooth, slightly-damp, spongy flesh. There were two particularly powerful ones entwined around her legs starting from the center of her calves and rushing all the way up to her thighs, and Lyeth did her best to try to keep them together with her impressive warrior's strength. Still, even she was unable to resist as the tentacles pried her legs apart and lifted her heels up into the air, just as others went for her arms. Like a sea of slithering snakes, Audrey's appendages continued to shiver across her, a wave of them cascading up Lyeth's back to grip over her shoulders, circle about her biceps, and work themselves into her palms to force her hands open.

The Daru went quiet, though the smile on her face wasn't just one of prideful delight but of a clear challenge. With a wordless gaze, she was offering herself up as a prize to be claimed, as if she were the dangerous, uncontrollable monster in the cave. The goblins that had just recently been evicted would be inclined to agree. While the mighty woman was further entangled, she kept resisting, making Audrey's extensions work for every inch that they spread her legs, forced apart her arms, and after just a few brief moments of flirtatious creeping, began to peel away the strips of leather that made the Daru's clothing.

"Ahh!" Lyeth was forced to gasp as a sudden bouquet of wriggling black and purple lengths snapped at the locks of her hair, twisting around until it formed a tight ponytail and yanked fiercely back. It exposed the Daru's throat, and yet another tentacle seized upon the opportunity, lashing against it with a wet slap complete with the popping noises that came with suction pads attaching to Lyeth's toned flesh. From there, the tentacle holding the warrior's throat gave a firm but secure squeeze just as the wriggling army finally lunged for the leather.

The heavy strip across Lyeth's chest was the first to go, snapped free and tossed carelessly to the wall of the cave to unleash a pair of truly tremendous, heavy breasts. In that brief moment, they were the *only* part of Lyeth that wasn't completely dominated by the writhing mass of shadowy lengths, swinging free and bouncing into perky place thanks to her incredible muscle tone. Stiff, dark nipples were left exposed and showcased perfectly just how excited the warrior was, and when Audrey's expansive sea of rubbery touches rushed for her, the Daru unleashed a moan through a constricted throat. Her hips bucked, and in doing so, she exposed more of her armor to the snagging and sneaky tentacles, which beared down across her body with a wild flurry.

Audrey's gaze was unflinching and without reaction as she stared ahead, watching without so much as a blush as her lover's layers were peeled away. She was reckless with

Lyeth's makeshift armor, and it was a foregone conclusion that some of the strips of otherwise-tough leather wouldn't be salvageable by the time morning came. That mountainous, glorious brute of a woman would have to make do under the light of the sun, wearing scraps torn asunder or strolling about in her bare glory. As the tentacles continued their relentless assault, more and more of Lyeth became exposed, but only for a brief few seconds; when leather was peeled away from her smooth, cream-colored flesh, it was quickly obscured once more by the grinding, writhing embrace of one of Audrey's creeping extensions.

The exception was the Daru woman's nethers, which were revealed fairly early into the onslaught but left unusually untouched. Below the leather cladding that once hung from her hips, Lyeth sported a nest of curly blonde hair much like that atop her head, proudly thick and untamed, leading to the faintest sight of a glistening, pink slit hiding just below it. The passion of the Daru was a famous thing amongst the people of Rugget, and whether their lusty interests were more inclined towards battle or the bedroom, they were known for an almost unchecked hunger. Lyeth personally leaned more towards the thrill of combat and the visceral joy of crushing her enemies below her, but this? This was clearly working for her as well, and her excitement grew every time one of those tentacles yanked at her arms or legs or forced her into a new position.

She fought it, of course. Not because she wished to escape the cave that night, but because of the rush of pleasure she felt as her muscles ached, and her lungs burned with each breath. Left exposed and swarmed, she was actively resisting as Audrey attempted to push her down to her knees, attempting to make her bear down on the ground like a submissive, loyal pet. As suction cup-clad tentacles lashed around her legs and drove one knee down into the dirt, Lyeth viciously resisted allowing the same fate to happen to the other and kept her foot braced while she tried with all her might to stand.

"Y...You...you won't…" Lyeth's grin was enormous, her eyes wide and flashing with fury, her cheeks a burning red. The tentacle bound around her throat, the dozens entwining her naked body, the loom shadow of Audrey's limp humanoid half - none of them were able to suppress her, and each ounce of pressure applied to the Daru only seemed to fuel her passion more. "You can try all night, but you'll never...break...me…"

Audrey, with a gesture that seemed as bold as any considering the woman's general emotionless state, simply tilted her head in response to Lyeth's words. And, almost as if she wanted to *immediately* prove her lover wrong, suddenly threw her up into the air.

"Woaaah, the fu-" Lyeth's face was one of absolute shock as she went from pinned and nearly prone by dozens of tentacles to completely airborne, launched almost as high as the short-sitting ceiling of the cave. For that brief fragment of a second, she was completely untouched by her partner, and in that moment, her impressive figure swung upside-down, nearly driving her head to the cold, unforgiving stone below. Thankfully for her, Audrey's tendrils seemed unlikely to allow that to happen, and like a pack of hungry eels, they all lunged forward once more to reclaim her. "F-Fuck, Audrey, that's cheating!"

Cheating or not, Lyeth found herself in a whole new form of helplessness as she was left dangling from the countless tentacles. They swarmed around her with a renewed vigor and shamelessly fondled her, with a particularly thick one weaving between her breasts as two small, lithe tendrils stretched forward to encircle the Daru's excited nipples. Lyeth was left under a constant state of stimulation as she was tipped backside over head, dangling upside down with her thighs spread and her arms stretched wide, all at the behest of her partner. Her hair was left dangling to the ground, and her head was swimming. For the first time, the brute was truly overwhelmed by it all. The writhing, the grinding, the slightly-damp embrace of those crawling appendages...they were everywhere. No joint on her body was left without a tentacle of some form nestled at the crook, no spot on her spine was left without a sucker pressed against her flesh, and no vacancy of note upon her impressive figure would be left without violation - as she soon discovered.

The powerful Daru, that mountain of a woman that made others quiver on the field of battle, went cross-eyed as a moan escaped from the back of her throat only to be muffled as one of Audrey's wriggling appendages pushed against her lips. It surged forward at the same time as two others of similar thickness curled up and around her thighs and squaring themselves against two sensitive entrances. The warrior's smoldering entrance was teased and tickled by a sucker-clad tendril that started to entreat entrance while her rear was similarly claimed, the latter taking a much more smooth, slippery unit.

While those swarming tendrils crept forward, Lyeth was left truly and delightfully helpless in the moment, so much so that she did something truly, truly rare for her: she gave up the fight. There was no more playful resistance, no more teasing challenge in her eyes. Such things could be secured away and enjoyed later, but for now? For now, the towering brute was happy to give in to the motions of her multi-tentacled lover.

Lyeth's eyes drifted close as her holes were steadily filled by writhing, wriggling masses that followed no orders but their own desires. Her mouth was claimed by a similar length that pushed well past her maw and pressed her tongue to the floor of her mouth, trembling back and forth before pushing even deeper. The spongey, slippery texture came with a flavor the warrior had difficulty discerning - a taste of smokey char almost reminiscent of standing inches away from a bonfire but with an oddly sweet hint that crept up upon her when the Daru's wide, flat tongue stroked across a particularly damp point of the tentacle's flesh. She rather enjoyed it, much as she delighted in the taste of dense sweat and spit that came in the midst of battle. An acquired taste, but one Lyeth could appreciate like few others.

While her mouth was filled, the tentacles pushing into her upturned entrances drove deep. While the humanoid half of Audrey paled in comparison to the nine-foot behemoth that was Lyeth, the tentacles that now stretched her entrances made it abundantly clear that the strange woman had no trouble in filling her. The warrior's rear entrance flinched and seized the invader as it pushed forward, at first trying to actively squeeze it out by pure muscular reaction, but Audrey was truly, insatiably, relentless. The tentacle probed deeper, drove harder, and all the while, it continued to excrete a thick, slimy nectar that made its invasion as smooth as could be. Before long, Audrey had worked more tentacles into Lyeth's backside than any tiny human or elf could ever hope to handle, and judging from the blank look on the warrior's rolled-back eyes, she was handling it with a hefty surge of depraved delight.

With her fiercest entrance claimed and her mouth muffled to the point of every moan whimpered within her throat, the tentacle teasing Lyeth's nethers finally grew bold. A few of the smaller ones suddenly whipped forward and padded their way through the gloriously thick blonde locks nearby, like creepy, boneless fingers weaving their way affectionately across her forest. As they did so, one of those 'fingers' stayed behind to pad at the sensitive pink flesh of Lyeth's hood, wiggling back and forth in between snapping with almost tail-like flicks, all while the strange digit slathered Lyeth's flesh in her slippery, clear glaze. Lyeth's muscles tightened, and her hips bucked against the iron-strong grip of Audrey's tentacles, pushing forward in a muffled desperation for more. The feet worth of tendrils dancing in her backside, the slippery unit moving deep down her throat, the creeping purple snakes teasing her hair...they were all gloriously satisfying, and in the very same breath, not nearly enough. And much to Lyeth's delight, it seemed as if Audrey agreed.

The tentacle she offered up to the warrior's nethers was something truly impressive indeed, and in the fleeting few seconds that Lyeth was able to see through the swarm, she bore witness to what was about to claim her. Thicker than the others, this particular tentacle had an oddly shaped head. Though it ended in a rounded tip like all the others, it was larger and wider and with a series of sporadic bumps spread across its surface, like the teeth of a morning star. It was that strange unit which now pushed against her entrance, squeezing to a hole that would need to stretch to accomodate. While it pushed against her, a secondary one that had been teasing Lyeth's entrance up to that point suddenly retreated, though it was bold enough to offer a sharp, wet slap across one of the warrior's thighs as it pulled back.

That studded head remained perfectly in place, just barely bridging the entrance to the upside-down Daru. The wiggling within Lyeth's mouth suddenly intensified as Audrey began to pull her muffling appendage back, just enough to pluck from the warrior's maw and leave Lyeth a stunned, shivering mess. Threads of dense spit dangled from the corners of her mouth and splattered into her hair; her face was fully overtaken by a wild blush, and it took her a few seconds to allow her eyes to properly focus. Once they did, however, Lyeth gave a sudden swallow of the excess glaze Audrey left within her throat and practically barked at the creature that now gazed at her with head tilted and pale features wearing the ghost of emotion.

"Stop playing with your prey and fuck it, already," the brute hissed, half-growled, and half-purred, her eyes flashing with a venomous, almost manic delight. Always one to push the limits, always one to lean on the side of crass and downright ferocious desire, she offered one final note to her wicked command towards Audrey. As the humanoid half of the creature loomed close, Lyeth reared her head back, pressed her lips tight together, and spit squarely into Audrey's pale face.

It was a combination of saliva and Audrey's own glistening secretion - the very same glaze that was making the ferociously deep penetration into Lyeth's backside tolerable and promised to do the same with the studded unit teasing her entrance. As it struck Audrey's face, the woman predictably didn't blink or flinch. The sheer size difference between their respective heads ensured that it was nearly enough to coat Audrey's entire colorless cheek, and as it slithered down over her flesh and dripped down to the robes below, Lyeth simply flashed that crazed, wild smile once more. Dangling upside down, threaded in her tightest hole, absolutely helpless...there was no state the Daru could be in that would stop her from reminding Audrey what a wild beast she was to tame.

And Audrey, much to the surprise of the curly-haired, blonde behemoth, actually responded. One of those limp arms suddenly animated with a wild twitch, and when it crept up from the elbow, it did so at an unnatural angle. While Lyeth's eyes drew wide and her mouth started to fall agape, Audrey brought her limp fingers up to the spit that glazed her cheek and pressed down against the flesh.

Her movements were unnatural - even more so than the rest of her. The tentacles that even now writhed and swarmed around Lyeth's body at least moved in a fluid fashion that seemed *normal* for such appendages. But the manner in which her hand twisted from her robe almost completely around, the way her curled fingers and twitching thumb crossed over her face, the way she ushered that glaze of spit into a mouth that was creeping open like a dark and menacing portal...it was unsettling even to a woman that had built her life upon the wreckage of bodies in the field of battle. Not even Lyeth, in all her time with the strange creature she shared her company with, had seen Audrey's humanoid form move so much. And as the creature held her mouth open, she revealed a tongue as black as night, dragging it forward and between her fingers, collecting the excess that Lyeth had provided. Once she did so, Audrey's mouth snapped closed again and her arm suddenly went dead, dropping like a felled tree to once more hang in a limp, motionless state before her.

And with that, Audrey spoke.

“My only hunger is for you.”

Her words were hoarse and only barely audible over the sound of her slippery, writhing tentacles grinding around each other and around the limbs of the Daru. Even worse, she only gave Lyeth precious few split-seconds to process what she said before all those thrashing appendages soon turned to a state of frenzy, most notably the one pressed against the warrior’s entrance, which finally pushed itself forward. Perhaps there was a time when Audrey would have afforded Lyeth the chance to slowly grow accustomed to the bulging unit pushing at her slit, an opportunity to brace herself for the stretch that was to come. If such a thought slipped through Audrey’s mind, it was clearly dashed away by the brute’s resilient nature and constant, almost instinctual desire to push things to a moment of fervent, desperate fury. Lyeth had proved that she didn’t desire any mercy...and she would not be shown any.

The Daru’s howl was suddenly snuffed out by the same tentacle that once occupied her mouth, again squeezing past her lips and pinning her tongue. This time, it probed even deeper, sweeping not just within her mouth but well into her throat, pushing forward with a thrashing, crawling insistence that Lyeth had no hope of combating. The Daru found a similar presence of authority and hunger twitching inside of her rear, and while Lyeth had managed to hold herself in check with that massive unit working within her while she was teased, now her walls were left convulsing and failing to grip the writhing, wriggling length that probed her desperately deep. But those penetrations - as unforgiving as they were and downright frightening to anyone that didn't have Lyeth's resolve - were but precursors to what pushed within her nethers.

That bulging, studded tentacle suddenly drove itself inside her with a fluid strike, forgoing any chance at playful foreplay during which Lyeth could prepare. Those tiny nodules dancing around the head dragged across her innermost walls, pushing well past the boundaries of what she could've expected from a more conventional lover. It pushed deep and mercilessly, stretching parts of the Daru that even she herself could only speculate upon, so completely addled and overwhelmed as she was. Lyeth's eyes crossed, and she continued to offer muffled moans against the tentacle pinning her tongue, and there she dangled helplessly in the embrace that she not only requested but deserved.

Hundreds had fallen before Lyeth of the Daru. Rare was the enemy that she couldn't conquer, and her years had been marked with victory earned through brutality, bravery, and a stubborn resolve that was stronger than steel. Even rarer still to the towering blonde was an ally that she could trust - especially to the extent that she gave herself over that night. In that moment of wild ferocity, Lyeth was left tumbling through the air, rolling up and down at the tightening call of endless tentacles, her holes claimed by a merciless affection that only gave her one option: to endure. Endure the strain of their sticky embrace as they pulled at her limbs, squeezed her joints, rode deep within her body, and bulged her throat and lap from the impact. Endure the sensory overload that came with every breath laced with the smokey flavor of Audrey's taste - when breaths were actually permitted to be stolen. Endure the feeling of suckers clinging to her flesh over sweat and goosebumps, of tendrils walking down her spine even as they threw her back and forth between each other's grasp, of a slimy, writhing tentacle wrapping tight around her throat.

And of course, endure what that moment of profound submission did to the most primal parts of the untamed Daru brute.

Underneath Audrey's gaze - which had by now returned to the same expressionless state - Lyeth gave in to her wicked pleasure. Her body convulsed and thrashed so hard that the tentacles were forced to tighten their grasp even as others scooped underneath her, helping to hold her weighty, muscular frame aloft. It was hard to tell, even for the Daru herself, when her climax truly began. The crawl towards her peak was one of intense and suffocating delight, trapped in a state of blissful helplessness that no other creature on Rugget could possibly force her into. Heat overcame her, and she wore both sweat and Audrey's clear, dense glaze like two extra sets of skin, her hair matted to her face and the bulge in her throat while that tentacle continued to surge forward. With her head swimming and her heart racing, with every muscle in her remarkable body taut and twitching, with any semblance of dominance long-since plunged from her, Lyeth hit her peak with a shameless joy.

The spasms that ran through her were so volatile that Audrey guided more tentacles to her figure, so many that the mighty Daru was practically left cocooned within them. Tiny ones wove between her fingers and others enwrapped her nipples just as large, flat-faced ones slapped back and forth across her breasts with loud, wet spanking noises. What was once a pair of thick black coils weaving along her legs soon became two and even three separate sets, working tightly against each other and covering up all traces of the woman's cream-colored flesh.

When Lyeth continued to thrash, so violently that she forced herself into yet another wild peak, her nethers wore proof of her pleasure in the form of a sudden squirt. Her own wild glaze filled the air in a juicy arc, rushing hot and wet through the air and splattering across the smooth, damp surfaces of Audrey's endless swarm. Some of it even managed to travel squarely to the creature's humanoid face - streaking over her pale features from brow to chin on the same side that Lyeth's spit crossed her. This time, Audrey didn't lift a hand to wipe it away; anybody would be hard pressed to argue that she wasn't doing enough already.

Lyeth's trapped and well-claimed figure continued to spasm like that as the tentacles continued their play, exploring her in ways that the Daru never thought possible. They jostled her back and forth and relentlessly pounded against her, and it wasn't long before she felt those appendages start to slither right back out. It was a brief respite offered in quick succession as her mouth, rear, and slit were both left free from contact - but only so long as it took for replacements to move into position. The studded, bulging tendril shifted to squeeze against her rear entrance while her nethers could soon feel *two* smoother tentacles weaving against it, entwining around each other like twisted candy before driving against her again. In the few seconds that her mouth was left vacant, Lyeth allowed her head to droop forward as she desperately gasped for breath, groaning and whimpering as the experience left her nearly broken within delight.

The only way she could tell that she had been positioned right-side up again was the fact that her thick blonde hair hung once more at the sides of her face, or at least, what wasn't matted against her scalp through a combination of sweat and Audrey's nectar. Long, thick threads of spit dangled in sloppy lines down the corners of Lyeth's mouth, oozing toward the ground and dancing with every breath that shuddered past her lips. Her vision was blurry, her heart was thundering in her chest, and even though the invading tendrils within her lower holes had temporarily ceased their motions, she could still *keenly* feel their presence.

The studs spread across the bulging unit wedged deep within her backside, and the coiled tentacles claimed her slit as if they were a pair of dancing snakes, a constant reminder that on that particular night, she belonged to Audrey. Whether as a travelling companion, a lover, or simply prey...it didn't matter, nor did Lyeth particularly care which. Whatever the role, it was one that objectively suited her.

Through the haze of heat and the exhaustion that she was desperately fighting against, Lyeth lifted her head to once more see the expressionless face of her partner. Audrey had positioned herself to stoop particularly close to her at that point, staring eye-to-eye and very nearly letting their noses touch. And while Lyeth's breath caused the threads of dark hair framing Audrey's face to dance and the beads of her own squirt to fall from the woman's pale cheek, there was no return force pushing against her. In fact, it didn't seem like Audrey was breathing at all.

"N...not so...bad out here..." Lyeth's voice was weak in that moment, worn from the tentacle that had probed her throat so roughly and from screams and moans left muffled against the same. Still, despite everything she had been through that night and with everything she was *still* enduring, she managed to meet Audrey's gaze with her own and force a small smile to crook at the corner of her spit-glazed lips. "...I guess."

The other woman didn't raise her hands to affectionately caress the face of her lover. Nor did she offer her sweet and tender words that would've been more appropriate for other, weaker, more conventional partners. Still, there was a single favor she extended to Lyeth in that moment that the Daru did not expect, and it came as the strange woman dipped forward a few short inches to bring their faces together.

The first touch of Audrey's lips against Lyeth's own were astonishingly cold - as chilling as ice and as smooth as the same. When those lips slowly began to part, Lyeth allowed her own to meet them, receiving the kiss in a fashion that was downright submissive considering her usual bravado. The Daru's weak voice offered a quiet whimper as she first felt the touch of Audrey's tongue against her own, filling her mouth with a familiar flavor as it explored and moved with a speed and precision that the rest of the woman's humanoid half simply lacked. And Lyeth, despite all her stubborn ferociousness, despite the tentacles still deeply exploring her and despite the ones still gripping her like iron, found herself doing something she had never done before: swooning. Her eyes closed, and her heart skipped a beat with emotions rushing through her that most would've assumed didn't belong in the core of a brutal warrior such as herself.

Although ultimately, with the two most dangerous women in Rugget, such moments of tenderness were fleeting; Lyeth soon realized that the slippery, writhing thing leading from Audrey's mouth and into her own was not, in fact, a tongue. The moment of sentimental connection was entirely consumed from that point as Audrey guided her most surprising tentacle past Lyeth's tongue and deep, *deep* within her throat. At the same instant the others all seized upon the warrior's flawless figure, and the ones claiming her nethers and rear began to play again, even more violently and vigorously than before.

And Lyeth, who would wake up in the morning sore like she'd never known before and covered with suction pad marks, gave in to it all. To the pull of Audrey's tentacles, to the passion of her intoxicatingly bizarre companion, and to the new life that laid ahead of them both.

It didn't matter how many homes she was exiled from, so long as Audrey stayed close as her shadow.

You lower the flask of Elfelpin Brandy, having finished it off during Glory's story. It's bitter but strong, without any trace of floral flavor or anything resembling sweetness. If a drink could be honest, that'd be it. Whoever designed such a drink - whether it was one person or a team of brewmasters - was to be commended for the most deadpan drink that ever touched your lips.

"Oh, and don't let the sweet story fool ya." It seems that Glory wasn't quite done with her story, and she points a firm finger square at your nose. "That Lyeth? A real pain in the ass. I could tell ya stories about that particular brand of bitch, that much is for sure."

Glory leaves you be after reaching out to snatch the flask from your hand, the same one that she had confiscated from the elf spy that sought to steal her secret brew in the first place. With a pleasant smile, she spins on a heel and goes right back to tending to the patrons, a line of which has started to form at the counter, waiting for her to finish her tale. It seems like nobody at the bar would ever dare whisper a wrong word to her for fear of getting tossed out on their backsides, but while she helps serve drinks to those at the front of the line, you can still hear whispers from the ones in the back.

"Every day with how much she hates that Lyeth woman."

"Can you blame her, after what she pulled?"

"I guess not," comes the murmured response, before a more thoughtful tone takes over. "Hey, whatever happened to the old bouncer? That shorter Daru with the huge cock?"

It's a good thing you've already pulled down the last swallow of Elfelpin Brandy, lest you accidentally choke on it.

"Dunno, but she was all kinds of fun." A brief pause follows in the conversation, until it continues just barely over the noise of the bar. "She fucked my wife once. Then me. Then us both at the same time. It was great."

With a cautious glance, you look back to the Daru woman that remains - the one that's still guarding the front door with a sharp, jealous eye while standing tall as a figure of imposing presence.

It's hard to imagine who could possibly make that titan at the door seem like a runner-up, but she'd have to be one amazing bitch indeed.

The Cute Boy Forest Bride

Chaotic noise fills the tavern from wall to wall, and you watched, stunned, as the scene unfolds. You've never seen so many adventurers move at once and utterly fail to capture their target. It's almost enough to shake one's faith in relying on freelancers for heroic assistance.

An elf with a longbow on her back lacks the hand-eye coordination to snag the glowing blur that's darting through the air in wild, erratic movements. Soon, it jumps high into the air only to immediately dive straight towards the floor, right in between the legs of the Daru bouncer that smacks her head off a table in an attempt to grab it. While that massive woman is still growling and rubbing her forehead, the blur of light shoots to the far end of the tavern and lands straight in the middle of a poker game played by a group of crowfolk, who all suddenly start squawking and pecking at the table, only adding to the noise filling the place.

"Get it! Get that damn thing and smash it!"

"Get back here, you obnoxious little rat!"

"CAW! CAW! CAAAAAW!"

By the time the flying ball of light and chaos reaches your end of the bar, you're already wincing from the noise. There are too many voices all calling out at once, too many patrons tripping over each other in a desperate bid to catch that wild ball of light. You're not even sure where it came from, but it seems absolutely determined to cause as much havoc as possible. The only person that seems unphased by the ensuing chase is the bar's mistress herself, who simply wears a deadpan expression as she reaches a hand underneath the counter and pulls out a bowl of peanuts.

You watch as she stretches out a hand to put the bowl right in the dead center of the bar and gives a sharp whistle, enough to rise even higher than the various voices screaming and yelling. As soon as she does so, the ball of light suddenly stops, and in that brief second, it moves slowly enough for you to catch sight of what lies underneath the glow. A pair of tiny legs. Pointed, grinning teeth. Glistening dragonfly wings, rapidly beating back and forth.

That glimpse of the creature only lasts for a fraction of a second before it darts right towards the bowl of peanuts, plunging into it like a cool pond on the hottest of days. While a wicked giggling fills the bar and peanut shells begin to pop from the edges of the bowl and dance across the counter, Glory's deadpan expression remains. She pinches the edge of it, walks it casually over to the window at the very edge of the bar, and throws the entire thing outside. Peanuts, bowl, and disturbance alike all go tumbling out, and she swiftly slams the window shut and locks the latch immediately after.

You're still holding your mug as she looks back across the bar at you and gives an irate grunt, her arms folding sternly across her chest as she does so.

"Pixies. They're a real fuckin' pain in the ass."

The Endless Nightmare Frst. Renowned not just within the lands of Rugget but the entire world over, it stood as a dark streak of blight and misery in an otherwise peaceful land. Provided someone ignored the Blight Pools, of course. And the Savage Hills. And Port Failu--

The Endless Nightmare Frst was *one* of the dark streaks of blight and misery in an otherwise peaceful land. The boundary of the woods that most normal travelers would encounter was easy to spot - a line of blackened trees with leaves of ashen gray, sturdy and thick with gnarled branches that twisted like the grasping fingers of a demon. The soil was dingy and stuck to the boots, the air was musty and stale, and even in the middle of the day, light refused to penetrate its canopy. One could understand why the person that named it the Endless Nightmare Frst left a letter out, as staying any longer than needed in that eerie place - whether physically or occupied in mere thought - was inadvisable.

Rumors of the forest were many, ranging from the simple farm legends told to children that wouldn't go to bed to stories of horror and true, unbridled terror. Brave warriors turned to whimpering cowards when told of its wicked nature around a crowded bar, listening to a particularly curvy and enticing bartender spin tales of captivating fright. It was important to remember, however, that danger could be found anywhere. It wasn't the sole domain of the Endless Nightmare Frst - not in a world where someone could go in any direction and find a grim demise between the teeth of a gnashing beast. And it was just as important to remember that the boundary of that blackened forest, with all its menace and gloom, was a border made even stronger by rumor-fueled fear.

After all, people drank more when they were scared, so a good ghost story made for thirsty patrons.

Sorrel was not brave. Nor was he strong, sturdy, skilled in combat, or particularly fleet-footed. Smaller in stature than his brothers and sister back in the Homestead, the young man was often overlooked when it came to tasks around the farm. He couldn't hope to throw around bales of hay with the surprising ease of his big sister, nor did he have the dexterity to shoe and train horses like his brothers. Sometimes, it seemed like from the very day he was born, he was destined to help his family in his own, unique way. And even now, as a young man in his early twenties and fresh from the place he once called home, Sorrel had his own way of doing things.

He wasn't brave, but he was careful. He wasn't strong, but he was clever. He wasn't skilled in battle, but he was studious. And he wasn't fleet-footed...but he was patient. So patient, in fact, that not even the shadows of the Endless Nightmare Frst could make him squirm.

For what was nearly the fourth week in a row now, deep within the reaches of that fabled place, Sorrel woke up with a yawn. The first thing he saw looming above his head was the same as it had been since the very first night: the relatively boring ceiling of his tiny leather tent. For a long moment, he laid flat underneath the covers of his bedroll, arms tucked underneath his head, idly staring up, chewing gently on his lip while he did so. Even if there was something interesting above him, he genuinely doubted that he could see it. The Endless Nightmare Frst was pretty accurate for the first half of its name, remaining constantly shrouded in darkness thanks to a strangely thick canopy. Especially within the confines of his tent, the young human could only barely see a few inches before his eyes and even less before he stretched a hand outward and reached for his glasses.

The young man's morning started just as it always did, awakening untouched and unharmed in one of the most famously dangerous places in all of Rugget. The same yawn escaped the back of his throat as he stretched, and the same crick in his back made him wince - perhaps because yet *again* he somehow managed to fall asleep on the same plum-sized rock at his camp. Before long, however, Sorrel had collected a small leather satchel from just beside his bed and scooped it up underneath his arm, moving up to his knees to emerge from the heavy flaps of his tent.

"Good morning, Enfy." He offered a sleepy smile to the forest itself as he moved to face yet another warning, his eyes half-lidded behind the rims of particularly large, round, owlish glasses. They perfectly framed bright green eyes with thick lashes and slender eyebrows, and framing *them* was a shoulder-length nest of thick blonde hair with untamed bangs. He had the sort of hair that could only come from a hastily chopped haircut from someone usually accustomed to grooming horse tails, now allowed to overgrow through weeks of detachment from the rest of the world. By that point in the morning, he was still blinking the sleep from his eyes as he slipped into a jacket resting on a nearby stump, one of rich forest green that seemed downright colorful and vibrant in comparison to the rest of the forest. Still, he let a warm smile dance further across his cute, soft, *heavily* freckled features, and once more greeted the woods with fondness. "And what did you leave for me today?"

As he asked it, Sorrel's hand dipped into one of the pockets of his heavy and baggy jacket, fingers closing around a tiny, spongy object before pulling it free. Within his palm sat a moldy gray mushroom with flecks of green and red - almost certainly poisonous, gross and sticky to the touch, but still enough to make him smile.

"I suppose this is better than the dead mouse." Sorrel chuckled, flicked the mushroom from his camp, and relaxed back on his haunches for the moment. As he sat there, he pulled the tiny leather sack into his lap and idly opened it up, recovering from it a hide-bound book overstuffed with pages and strips of parchment. As the book flipped open within his palm and he pulled a pencil into his left hand, Sorrel paused, took a deep breath, and murmured idly to himself. "Let's see...day...thirty-four."

As Sorrel started to write, he sat completely fearless against the surroundings that would've caused other, braver people to shudder. Trees loomed so far above him and twisted together so intricately that looking upwards could cause an almost instant case of vertigo, and gazing down at the threads of black grass for too long could've easily convinced someone that they were actually a sea of writhing, dagger-headed worms. Taking too deep a breath would force an adventurer's nose to pick up the scent of rot and decay, and listening too keenly offered an array of horrors from the sticky, flopping drip of bubbling tar to devious whispers punctuated by random, deeper laughs. The Endless Nightmare Frst was not a place that held up to scrutiny, and so Sorrel simply...didn't scrutinize it, and instead casually talked along with the words he scribbled in his book.

"I still have yet to see actual proof of any of the famous threats of this place," he murmured, not *particularly* loud, lest his words offer the woods some offense. "Or at least, I have yet to truly experience it. Last night, my camp was assaulted by a horde of skeletons. I could hear their clattering bones approaching the tent, and when I peeked my head out, my eyes fell on each and every one. There were dozens of them, flesh dripping from their bones and mouths opening and closing as they spoke in a language I cannot identify." Sorrel paused, took a deep breath, and tapped his closed lips with the butt of his pencil. "So, I brought my dinner outside, and I offered them some. They declined, presumably either because they don't like iron boar jerky...or because they didn't really exist. If I'm being entirely honest, I'd believe either. The jerky is certainly fine, but I could use something different for a change."

With that, Sorrel closed his book once more, tucked it into the tiny leather sack, and slowly lifted himself up to his feet. From there, he drew the sack's strap across his shoulder and rocked back and forth on his heels, affording himself the first proper stretch of the morning. He was a slender young man, chest smooth and flat and waist angling inwards just a bit. Round, tiny shoulders flanked a short and skinny neck, one that was almost always half-hidden by the untamed locks of thick, soft blonde hair that drooped below his chin. The tiniest of the family for sure, but then also the only one of his siblings that had such a generous distribution of freckles. A fair tradeoff.

"I think I'll make a supply trip today, Enfy." Sorrel spoke aloud to seemingly no one in particular yet made sure his voice was high enough to catch against the dark leaves of the Endless Nightmare Frst. "Would you like me to bring you anything? Anything at all?"

There was silence in response, but admittedly, Sorrel didn't listen *too* hard. Such things were dangerous in this devious place.

"Well...I imagine it'll be a few hours before I reach the border," Sorrel continued to speak as he walked, his voice light and carefree even as he stepped over a barbed, thick vine that was actively moving as if it was attempting to grasp him. "If you think of something, let me know! And if not...well...maybe I can surprise you?"

Sorrel continued to march through the most famously frightening spot in all of Rugget and perhaps even all of Sombfal. The dangers of the world beyond the woods were easy to spot - the bubbling green and red sludge of the Bile Pools, the shifting sand that precluded the appearance of a Felpin scarab boat, the smoldering, sparking breath of a combustion dragon. But the Endless Nightmare First simply didn't work like other places, as Sorrel had learned so many days into his stay.

Enfy did things Enfy's way - and like any polite visitor, Sorrel respected that.

***

They were rare, but there were still a few small settlements near the border to the Endless Nightmare Frst. Driven by desperation rather than bravery, anyone that set down that close to such a storied place was doing so because the greater comforts of the Homestead or Clover were no longer available to them. As such, when someone like Sorrel - cute and small, friendly and polite - approached their makeshift towns, he was almost instantly targeted for some sort of larceny. Seeming easy to take advantage of and even easier to bully, those shady rogues hiding out in the shadow of the wicked woods almost immediately identified him as a tender and vulnerable target.

At least, of course, until they pieced it together that the boy approached them from the *direction* of the Endless Nightmare Frst, and as such, showed him the proper respect.

This was one such trip that morning, and Sorrel was once more surprised at the sheer friendliness of the people of the quasi-settlement. Everyone smiled broadly upon seeing him and even offered him quite the deal for his supplies - everything from flint and tinder to a fresh set of cleaning cloths, a bottle of horse trough-made wine, and few more meals' worth of food. Usually, Sorrel had to make do with various types of jerky - it seemed sometimes like it was *all* that the people on the fringes of the settlement ate - but that particular day he was overjoyed to have purchased a heaping sack of bright, colorful oranges. One of the 'merchants' had most likely robbed a nearby Homestead farm in the night.

Regardless, Sorrel had a spring in his step as he marched right back into the darkness of the Endless Nightmare Frst, much to the shock and surprise of the people in the makeshift settlement. No doubt they'd only further build upon the legend of that place after that day, stories of a mysterious ghost boy that wandered from the woods in search of fruit, freckled and friendly and with a soft grace about him. The stories would probably build upon each retelling until eventually Sorrel's mouth drew wide enough to swallow a wagon with eyes burning violent and red as his body went translucent. But such tales weren't to be believed. Mostly, he just said a lot of pleases and thank-yous.

And now, while he walked through the darkness of the woods, Sorrel was tucking a hand into the fresh sack of oranges and plucking one out and into his palm. The sheer color of the thing was a stark contrast to the rest of the grim world beyond, with trees and leaves as dark as pitch and wisps of rolling, flameless cinders constantly drifting in the air. That sudden burst of color was downright jarring, even disorienting as Sorrel tossed it up and into the air before catching it into his outstretched palm. Idly, the young man hummed to himself while he pressed onward back to his camp, casually throwing the orange aloft and catching it in his palm. Again and again, with the melody of his hum rising, up it went and down it came...until at a certain point, it failed in the latter half of the equation.

Sorrel paused, the fingers of his outstretched palm shifting and closing within his hand before opening up again. He didn't bother to look up - as if he'd fall for such a playful, disorienting trick from the forest - but he did give a soft chuckle before speaking aloud with his usual friendly, almost doting voice.

"You could've asked if you're hungry, Enfy," he murmured, and then slipped his hand back into his sack to pull free yet another orange. "But that's okay. I bought plenty to spare."

He gave out plenty of oranges by the time he returned to camp. Two more were lost as he threw them up into the air in a friendly game while a third was simply left on a stump and had vanished by the time he looked back at it. Another one was dropped off in the center of a ring of sticky-looking rocks that were *not* there on his first time through the woods that morning, while the fifth was deposited in a low-sitting bird's nest that didn't have any eggs but still offered a suspiciously orange-shaped divot. Sorrel just smiled each time he gave a new offering, his sack of oranges getting lighter and lighter, and before long, he reached into his bag and realized he'd wrapped his fingers around the very last one. With that single last flash of color firmly held within his palm, Sorrel upturned the now-empty bag to show Enfy that the treats were running low.

"This one's mine," Sorrel announced since it was important to take a stand with the Endless Nightmare Frst. After all, if he didn't, the place would walk all over him! "But I might be convinced to share...if you show up in person and ask me to."

With that, Sorrel held the single orange close as he pressed onward, musing to himself not only about Enfy's fascination with the fruit, but with all the dark, grim rumors about this place. Everyone back in the Homestead - his family included - was sure that the Endless Nightmare Frst was a place where the undead held dominion. A place of boundless horror and, well, nightmares. Even as a child, he never quite believed those tales, and now as an adult he believed them even less. Sure, he had *seen* undead like the skeletons the night previous, the rotting corpses that dangled from the trees like spider monkeys on the second week, the body of a long, serpentine ghost that crawled through the brush glowing with blue and ominous light...but seeing wasn't always experiencing. And while he first entered these dark woods in the hopes of finding something that might bring his family some level of renown, these days?

These days, he stayed because he liked the company. And naturally, he was excited when he returned to his camp only to discover that he was finally about to meet his host in person. Or hosts, as the case may be.

Sorrel was still protectively holding that single remaining orange by the time he saw the tip of his tent just over the horizon. At that point in his walk, he was fully expecting to sit out in front of it and enjoy the meal all by himself, firmly expecting Enfy to remain quiet until the evening at which point the nightmarish images and horrendous shrieking noises would emerge as they always did. But when he stepped just high enough to peer towards the floor of the hillside, Sorrel was left completely dumbstruck. For the first time since he'd stepped foot in that strange place, he saw a flash of color that was *not* one he brought with him.

Lightly frosted blue hair. Flesh of a deep, almost smoky pink. Wings like those of a dragonfly, only glittering with a beautiful, frolicking yellow.

Also, segmented black insect eyes and wide mouths with jagged, jack-o-lantern-esque mouths. Because even if Enfy was pretty...Enfy was still creepy.

There were at least ten of them, and when the young man finally stood within a dozen feet of his tent, they all turned to look at him with looks that he could only presume were curious. Tiny heads tilted, wide mouths either beaming from ear to pointed ear or gnashing like they were trying to chase him off. It was a tiny army of pixies that now collectively turned their attention upon him, gazing ahead with a level of intrigue that Sorrel certainly matched. The boy's eyes went wide, and his throat tightened, his nerves instantly set into a state of wild, uncontrolled rattling. Not because he was afraid, of course, but because he was certain that this was the moment that he'd finally be meeting his neighbors.

"It's very nice to finally meet you." The young man offered a small and polite bow to the group, one hand closing over his chest and the other still holding his orange close at hand. "My name is Sorrel. Do...any of you speak the human tongue?"

"Sorrel! Sorrel! I told you his name was Sorrel!"

"'Allo, hunam!"

"Fruit fruit fruit fruit fruit ahhhhhhh I love fruit so much--"

"He's pretty in person! Pretty pretty pretty!"

"What're those dots on his face? What's that big sniffy thing above his mouth?"

"Hunam, 'allo!"

"POCKETS. POCKETS. POCKETS."

"Skeletons! We should make more skeletons! He liked those!"

"I told you he'd like my bird nest!"

"No, it was that dead mouse I gave him!"

"Hunam, 'allo, hunam!"

"Ask him to marry us! MARRY THE WOODS FOREVER AND DESPAIR, HUNAM. BECOME OUR CUTE BOY BRIDE."

"Shhh shhh SHUSH, you're gonna ruin it!"

The voices, much like the pixies themselves, all rushed upon Sorrel in a sudden storm. Each of the little things - and Sorrel was not so sure anymore that it was merely ten - took immediate flight and descended upon the young man like a flock of birds on a morsel of bread. From the sudden proximity, Sorrel could see the pixies much more clearly, and even though they advanced upon him with tremendous speed and intensity, he could get a better look at just how strange the tiny things were.

They were uniform in their colors - all with the same deep, smoldering pink like the inside of a dried strawberry. Their hair was all the same frosted and soft blue tint, though the styles varied greatly, from long trails hanging down over one's wings and to their backside to one with a short tuft at both sides in tiny pigtails. Another's hair was rich and filled with volume from all sides while another had, appropriately enough, a pixie cut. There was a great variety in how their hair sat against their heads but the same couldn't be said about their faces, with each one perfectly identical outside of the expressions they were making.

They had an eerie look to them, objectively so, and even to the curious young man now swarmed by them. None of the pixies seemed to have a nose, and it was hard to imagine they had the real estate to grow one considering matching sets of two large, solid black, segmented eyes like those of a horsefly. Their mouths didn't seem to sport teeth so much as points carved into the front of their faces, and each one grinned with a jagged, sharp maw as if they were carved from a pumpkin's face. Barefoot and garbed in long dresses of flowing white, the texture of which Sorrel couldn't even hope to guess, glowing wings lifted the pixies as they began to explore their visitor. Some of them flapped said wings with the effort of a hummingbird while others didn't move theirs at all, and indeed it seemed like the decision to do so was completely irrelevant to how high or how long they could fly.

The noise of their questions and sharp, piercing voices continued like the buzzing of a swarm as they suddenly rushed him. Sorrel simply raised his arms in a friendly gesture, his fingers still taut around the orange as the pixies, quite simply, explored him. One dipped into the pocket of his jacket and began thrashing around like a trapped mouse as another landed squarely on his head, just long enough to give a loud yawn before scooping an arm around some of his bangs and tucking itself in like for a presumable nap. One seemed completely transfixed upon the large black button at the front of his clothes and another perched on his shoulder with a smile - just another six-inch tall, weightless creature for him to hold aloft. He could feel the squirming of a pixie below his shirt and another pulling on his ear, and a quick glance down revealed one of them was prodding at his foot as if to make sense of the heavy leather boots he wore. With so many hands prodding him and so many voices trying to engage in unison, it was understandable that Sorrel felt briefly overwhelmed, and he couldn't help but laugh as he shivered from side to side and bucked his hips to displace one of the pixies that was trying to open the front flap of his pants.

"H-hey! All right, all right, that tickles!" Despite the fact that the creatures clearly had no concept of personal space or even the fact that they had only just met, he made an attempt to draw their attention away from their new fascination. Even in doing so, he was smiling from ear to ear; this was the experience he'd been hoping for since arriving in the Endless Nightmare Frst! Well...maybe not *exactly,* but it was still much better than the skeletons! "Are you the ones that have been causing all those illusions? The ones trying to scare me off?"

"Scare? What's scare?"

"I told you he wouldn't like the angry demon moose!"

"Well, I told *you* he wouldn't like the blood fountain!"

"PANTS. PANTS. PANTS."

"'Allo, hunam!"

"Illusions? LIFE IS AN ILLUSION, CUTE BOY BRIDE."

Amidst the noise one, of the pixies swung close to Sorrel's face, flitting from the crowd and forcing his eyes upon it. Just like all of them, the slip of a thing was tiny and elegant in a certain creepy way - graceful, with soft blue hair shaved down to the point that it was little more than a fuzzy stubble across that rich pink scalp. Smiling broadly to Sorrel, they spoke with a voice that was loud enough for him to pick up over the rest of the noise, grinning as they did so with that jagged, intimidating mouth.

"We have been here for centuries, making so many friends! In hundreds of years, we have made…" The pixie paused, counted on its fingers, counted a little *more* on its fingers, and then did some deeper calculations in its head. "Two friends! You're the best one yet!"

Sorrel laughed a little, and a blush rose underneath his freckled features. Rubbing a hand at the back of his head, he couldn't help but offer a somewhat shy response to that; he'd always been told he made a good listener! Still, due diligence was called for, and he allowed his voice to slip past his lips in a way as...non accusatory as possible. "And...this other friend," he began, carefully. "What did you...do with them?"

A strange question, perhaps, but in his defense, one of the pixies *was* trying to bite his arm. Thankfully, those little face-sculpted teeth weren't as dangerous as they looked.

"They left! Grumpy, that one! So grouchy, always yelling, always punching!" the pixie in front of Sorrel responded and shrugged. "One of us left with her! But they...well...they were the *worst* one. Will not be missed!"

"Nope, nope, nope!"

"Let them marry gross green hunam if they want!"

"Wait, which one was it? I forget!"

"You know, the *worst* one!"

"You gonna eat that fruit or what?"

"Wanna see a magic trick?"

"No, don't! He didn't like the dragon ghost! You're gonna scare him off!"

"SCARE OFF CUTE BOY BRIDE, AND I WILL BURN THE WORLD TO ASH."

Sorrel looked at the crowd of pixies and smiled once more, his shoulders lifting and his hands dropping to his hips. He rose the one that still held that big, bright orange, and as soon as he did so, one of the pixies slammed against it like a charging iron boar. While they all continued to play and swarm, another of the pixies brought itself up to Sorrel's line of sight, waving for him to follow while reaching out and grabbing a fistful of his blonde locks, pulling it like a leash.

"Come and celebrate! Celebrate with us! Celebrate meeting us!"

Naturally, its words caused the chorus to start anew.

"Our home is not so pretty, but hunam is welcome!"

"Take off your jacket! Don't worry about that big shiny button! I'll make sure it doesn't go anywhere!"

"New friend, new friend, Sorrel is new best friend!"

"FACE DOTS. FACE DOTS. FACE DOTS."

"We'll suck your great big human cock!"

Sorrel - and *almost* all of the pixies suddenly stopped dead in their tracks - and all of their heads turned to look at one of them in particular. It was the same one that was trying to get into his pants just a little bit ago and was now floating before his fly and gazing straight back at everyone else. With a frosted blue mohawk and the same segmented black eyes, they offered an indignant expression and shrugged their shoulders while their voice once more rose among the crowd.

"What? We were *all* thinking it!"

***

Sorrel was at a loss for words. Pulled along by what was essentially a cloud of countless pixies, the young man was yanked through the most condensed part of the Endless Nightmare Frst, physically nudged and shoved between the trees when they grew unnaturally close together and forced to hold his arms in front of his face as the branches and twigs nipped at it. It was a bit of rough treatment while the pixies rolled him along like kittens all playing with the same ball of yarn, and when he finally emerged at their destination, his eyes opened wide and his throat went comparatively tight.

There was...color! So many beautiful, vivid, breathtaking colors! The dark shroud of the Endless Nightmare Frst was still there, but only in the form of a fence around what was a shocking grotto of glory and peace. Like the muted colors in the background of a matte painting, the forest's dark canopy was easy enough to ignore as Sorrel's eyes danced across what was easily the most soothing spot he'd ever witness. Overtaken with a comforting blue glow, he stood among waist high flowers of bright and charming greens and yellows with the occasional plump red rose peeking through. Thick bushes sported strange plants that looked like twisting streamers of a glittering yellow, and in the very center of the grotto sat a pond with clear water and a few precious lilies floating on the surface. The water itself was slowly bubbling from below, just enough to make those petals dance and a faint steam escaped from its surface to suggest that it was naturally heated. And if Sorrel squinted and stared hard enough - something he normally *never* would have done in the tricky Endless Nightmare Frst - he could just faintly see the image of a rainbow hanging over the pool's surface.

But of course, with this particular group of hosts, he wasn't afforded much chance to stare and study.

"He hasn't said anything! I bet he thinks it's ugly!"

"He's just being polite! I bet he thinks *you're* ugly!"

"Into the water! It's nice and warm! Even hunams like nice and warm, right?!"

"Hunams like dark and cold and spooky! Quick, turn the water into sludge! *Bug sludge!*"

"N-No! No, don't change it!" Sorrel finally managed to speak up, holding up his hands as he stumbled forward. He was so eager to stop the pixies before they did anything brash that he didn't even notice they were all working in concert to loosen his clothing, teasing down the buttons of his jacket while rolling his sleeves further up his arms. He looked at the mass of eager little things and did his best to speak in a comforting tone, his eyes softening while he pushed his most diplomatic voice forward. "This is absolutely lovely. I like it here much better than...than out there."

With a single hand, he gestured to the black wall of the forest behind him, and the pixies all gave a gasp in collective shock. Some of them peeled away from his body so swiftly that it pulled his jacket and shirt below open, leaving his smooth, flat, hairless chest exposed to what was comfortably warm air. Once again, the chorus began in concert, a dozen voices speaking at once amidst their ranks.

"Told you, silly; he likes this! What a strange hunam!"

"Gross green hunam didn't!"

"Gross green hunam can suck my pixie ass!"

"Ask if he wants to bathe! Ask if he wants us to play with him!"

"DEMAND THAT HE BECOMES OUR CUTE BOY BRIDE."

"Ask about Enfy! Enfy this, Enfy that, who's Enfy?!"

"O-Oh! Oh, I can answer that," Sorrel finally spoke up again, stepping forward again. While he did so, he even allowed his hands to slip up to the collar of his jacket and shirt to begin peeling them away further, more than happy to go along with whatever the pixies had in mind. (Even though, in a fairly innocent farmboy fashion, he *still* wasn't sure entirely what all that was.) While he dropped his jacket to the smooth ground below one of the pixies went wild with wiggles, shooting into the fabric like a falling star to begin groping at that big, shiny button that was at the front of it. Sorrel ignored the noise as best as he could, addressing the others fondly. "Enfy is...well...it's what I've been calling the forest. My people - uh, hunams - call your home the Endless Nightmare Frst. And while I was here, it helped me if I...talked to the forest."

As he spoke, he couldn't help but realize how silly it all sounded - at least until the pixies offered their response. Giggles and cheers and clapping followed the young man's explanation, with one of the crowd flitting forward with arms outstretched to give the human a hug. Or at least, the rough equivalent of one as they pressed up against his cheek and wiggled back and forth.

"Enfy! Enfy! We're Enfy! We've always been Enfy!"

"Enfy! Enfy! Enfy!"

"Hooray! Enfy loves fruit!"

"ENFY DEMANDS TRIBUTE!"

The name filled the air like a melody, so much so that Sorrel found himself laughing as they once again coalesced around him. This time, however, the pixies were pushing against him even more aggressively than before. The hugs and the prodding were offered with more demanding pressure, and the tiny hands moving over his body weren't quite so gentle or innocent - nor were the bare feet walking down his spine or the first glimpse of an acorn-sized head pressing a kiss against his throat. Then another. And another. And a few more in rapid succession, from his neck to his shoulder to down his hairless chest, with one pressing just behind his earlobe in a sudden flurry of attention.

Sorrel blinked, one eye twitching from the unexpected affection offensive. The pixies had said some pretty shocking things already, but now that they all moved in tandem, it was a bit strange to experience let alone dwell on the notion that so many of them were becoming so intimate so very, very quickly. Sorrel couldn't help but blush as some of them dipped down to the belt of his baggy trousers and started to pull it free, and this time when they teased at the fabric, he didn't find himself pushing them away.

They were bold, certainly. They were demanding, absolutely. But much like the Endless Nightmare Frst they called home, it seemed like the only person that could truly be patient enough for them was the sweet son of horse ranchers and onion farmers, now marked with goosebumps and a heavy blush spreading underneath his freckles. Sorrel moved a hand up to make sure his glasses remained secure when one of the pixies tried to pluck them off - pushing his forefinger against the piece crossing the bridge of his nose to nudge it into place. When the pixie looked at him with confusion and maybe even a bit of dejected pouting, Sorrel just tapped one of the lenses and offered a kind smile.

"I need these," he explained. "I can't see without them, and...and you're all...so beautiful."

He looked down at his own body now, where more than a dozen pixies were looking straight back up at him with broad smiles fixed upon their jack-o-lantern-esque faces. Large, lidless, segmented eyes were shining with what could only be joy, and it looked like even their rich pink cheeks had somehow gained intensity for a blush. They were beautiful indeed. Mysterious, frantic, wild, completely eschewing any trace of polite behavior...but beautiful.

Creepy, too, but the pixies weren't *entirely* wrong about humans.

Sometimes, they liked spooky.

It was a strange sensation spread across several different ways as Sorrel sunk down into the waters of the grotto's pool. He was immediately struck by the warmth that splashed against him as if trying to invite him further, and when his smooth, bare backside landed, he found himself teased by surging, bubbling waters from unpredictable angles and locations. A surge across his waist, a line drawn over his spine, a tickle just below his undercarriage...it was a pool unlike any he had ever sat in, and he was left contending with it while at the same time feeling the swarm of pixies dance across his flesh. Left completely bare, the young man leaned back in an effectively prone state, groaning as he gave in to the charms of the Endless Nightmare Frst. Of Enfy.

"Ahh..hahh…" His voice escaped amidst a desperate breath just as his hips lifted from the stone and fell back once more. Generally speaking, he wasn't a man that found himself bare under the eyes of others very often in his life. Sure, there had been flirtations back home with visiting merchants or the random Daru that deserved a special "thank you" for a hero's job well done, but this was unlike anything he'd experienced ever before. The tiny bodies that crawled across his flesh were worshipping him with kisses and caresses, and as the moments continued, their tiny dresses all seemed to be cast aside. Some were ripped from their bodies amidst a wild giggle and ferocious if tiny roar, while others simply...vanished, leaving their owners bare underneath the gaze of the human.

And a bare pixie was indeed an intriguing sight. As Sorrel lifted an eye behind his glasses, he had the chance to study one that was floating particularly close, resting as it was upon his shoulder and dragging its naked figure across his body. It had the angles of a human but lacked the finer details; while wearing its robe it *looked* like it had a human's breasts considering the slope of their chest, but once that garment vanished, Sorrel could tell it was completely smooth underneath. No tiny bust, no separate pectoral muscles, not even the faintest hint of dark pixie nipples. Their nethers were quite the same, sporting neither a slit nor a shaft between a pair of smooth legs, where there was simply a continuation of smooth, seamless flesh. Regardless, the tiny creature was clearly excited even if they lacked the parts to show it, looking up at Sorrel and practically humming with pleasure, dragging tiny hands across his shoulder, and reaching towards his bushy, untamed blonde bangs.

When Sorrel let his eyes dance upon the crowd, he saw that they all sported similar bodies. Devoid of any of the usual hallmarks of human desire, yet completely overtaken by it. The only difference between them seemed to be the style of their light blue hair or when listening to the voices that rose amidst the flurry of attention they offered to him.

"Scrub, scrub, clean, clean! Clean Sorrel is happy Sorrel!"

"FACE DOTS, FACE DOTS, I LOVE SORREL'S FACE DOTS."

"Hunam is so smooth and pretty! Like a flower! Sexy, sexy flower!"

"Sorrel if you don't want this button, I can take it off your jacket for you!"

"Hey, look what I found!"

"Gyah!" Sorrel practically leapt up and out of the water as he felt another rush of attention at a particularly sensitive spot, a pixie burying themselves against the hanging sack and stiffening member between his thighs. After his initial surprise, he groaned with a growing excitement, forcing his teeth down against his bottom lip for an admittedly nervous nibble. This was the *last* thing he had expected to be doing when he finally discovered the secret of the Endless Nightmare Frst, but then...what a reward it was! Pleasure was already pushing through his body as more and more pixies got in on the action, one by one darting down below the surface of the enchantingly warm water to see what all the fuss was about.

He could still hear their happy voices from below the surface, and naturally, felt their arms and bodies move to embrace him. While one of the young man's eyes started to twitch from his poor senses being completely overwhelmed, the gang treated him to the sort of pleasure that no human had likely ever known. Slender, tiny arms wrapping around his stiffening shaft to give it a hungry squeeze. An acorn-sized head nuzzling his sack at the spot where it met his member. A chorus of pixies letting their arms and legs grind and explore across his undercarriage, and even a pair of tiny hands reaching out to rub at his tightly-spasming backdoor.

Though the joy Sorre was bringing them was not entirely the privilege of the pixies below the surface, for the ones that lingered above were still having the time of their lives.

"Look at his face! He likes us so much!"

"Psst, tell him I think he's cute! Do it, do it!"

"Look at these! What are *these* doing?!"

Sorrel actively squeaked as the pixies launched forward, two for each bud racing towards his nipples. They were showing the same levels of excitement as his throbbing length below the surface, and similarly, the enchanting tiny things were determined to bathe them in pleasure. For the first time, he could keenly feel little tongues crossing over his flesh, just as their hands massaged the sensitive areolas of his otherwise smooth, flat chest. It was clear that there was no part of this adventurous young man that the pixies wouldn't find some way to enjoy, and so it wasn't entirely a surprise when one of them floated forward. They had long blue hair framing their face all the way down to their shoulders, and though they sported the same exact face as the others, with the way their segmented eyes were bending inward, they looked almost...shy. Nervous, even.

"Uhm, uh...uhm...S-Sorrel…" they began, fidgeting, squirming, beating their tiny wings in rapid succession. "Could I...could I maybe...please…"

Sorrel was still at a loss, though desperately wanted to pay this particular pixie the attention they deserved. Even with all the other pixies scrambling across his length, he made sure to give them as much focus as he could muster and even managed to squeak out a few words amidst the sharp, aroused breaths. "A-Anything you like, I'm sure I'd be happy t--mmph!"

The human suddenly went cross eyed as the pixie acted on his words almost immediately, charging forward like a shot and swinging their back half forward just before making contact with his mouth. The pixie sunk into the young man's open maw as if it were a hot bath, their legs moving to dance across his tongue while her waist was left hugged by his lips. Sitting half within, the adorable thing offered a sudden, wild giggle, swiveling back and forth and allowing their voice to float into a joyous moan.

"Ohh, that's...that's so wonderful!" they called out, just as the sweet, fruity flavor of their lower half filled Sorrel's senses. A pleasant taste to be sure, once he managed to get past the shock of its source. While the pixie swivelled around within his mouth, they drummed their arms against his lips and even stretched out their hands to hold onto his nose, tugging at it like it was the hilt of a saddle. "G-Goodness gosh gracious! More, more, more!"

If Sorrel was in *any* position to really think about things, he would've found himself wondering just what pleasure the pixie was taking from the contact of his tongue between their tiny legs when they didn't actually *have* anything there. As luck would have it, such introspection wasn't afforded him as the other pixies were still constantly in motion, playing with his length that was growing harder and longer below the surface of the water. Two of them were sandwiching his member between their naked bodies, hugging each other as they grinded back and forth. Another four were all spending time at his sack to offer hints of affection within the warm, bubbling water. He wasn't sure how many of them were playing with his rear pucker, but it was *definitely* more than two, and when he finally looked down to see his tip peek out from the surface of the pool, yet another pixie darted straight to the tip.

"Whee, hehehe!"

They landed atop him with a surprising strength, notching their knees against the glistening pink head and tucking their tiny feet at the point where the tip met the shaft. From there, they bucked back and forth while the other two grinded at the sides, waving their hands through the air and shouting with reckless, loud, joyous delight.

Sorrel...didn't have a chance. Even putting aside the fact that he'd been in the Endless Nightmare Frst for weeks without any semblance of sensual comfort, this surge of attention was more than he could've resisted on his very best day. With a racing heart, he offered a sharp groan into the open air, only slightly muffled by a shivering backside of a quivering pink pixie lodged half within his mouth. It was simply too much for him. Too much attention, too much praise, too many tiny hands tickling his rump and too many kisses spread across his glistening tip. With another sharp moan, his hips bucked forward, rising briefly from the water as it splashed around. In that moment, his peak struck him like lightning, and the young man's twitching member convulsed, shuddering between naked pixie forms before shooting straight up into the air.

Or, at least it would have, if a pixie wasn't riding his tip at the point of release. That particular fae went spiraling up into the air like they'd just tried to fly into a wind current, giving a surprised yelp as they tumbled wings over rear with a jet of thick white cream chasing her. The pixies, predictably so, went absolutely wild as Sorrel hit his peak, and the entire nest of the surprisingly friendly things buzzed with voices and pleasure.

"Gimme! Gimme gimme gimme!"

"Noooooo, you broke him!"

"He's not broken! Look, he's smiling!"

"Hey, for real, are you *sure* you need this button?"

"It's sticky! It's heavy! It's...it's...wow! It tastes *so* good!"

Sorrel's eyes magnified, the corner of his lips twitching as he stared straight ahead at the sudden swarm. His hips were left hanging in the air as nearly every pixie *immediately* abandoned his body, shooting straight for the streaks of white cream even while he was still shooting them. Like a pack of instinct-driven birds, they swept through the jets of the human's release, nabbing it in mid-air and shoving heaping handfuls of it into their strange, jagged mouths. Watching his load be claimed in such a manner was...admittedly a bit unnerving, but Sorrel couldn't comment. After all, the only remaining pixie was the one that was still hanging half out of his mouth, their own fruity backside pressed up against his tongue. They even looked back over their shoulder and folded their arms across their chest in a mock pout.

"Why'd you stop? My fairy butt won't lick itself!"

"It did that one time!" one of the others called out just before jamming a heaping mountain of human seed into their mouth and messily slurping.

Sorrel, with his tongue trembling and his body already weakening, merely grunted and collapsed back into the pool with a weary, but quite satisfied smile on his face.

After his climax and the pixie's subsequent feeding frenzy, the young man was surprised to find that the pace of things slowed down - at least long enough for him to collect his thoughts. The swarm of those friendly little things moved away from intimate notions while their meals settled, and instead of fawning over their visitor with lewd demands, they actually started to scrub him clean. Dozens of sets of hands set to work upon him in a half-bath and half-massage, and while one of them perched atop his shoulder, the others all remained diligent, humming to themselves and occasionally chiming in with their own errant thoughts.

And Sorrel had to admit, it was nice. A stark difference from his previous nights in the Endless Nightmare Frst where illusions would be attempting to force him out, and certainly better than the lonely nights when he didn't even have the scary light show to keep him company. As he stretched back within the pool and rested his arms against the stone, the young man gave a satisfied and happy sigh. And when his glasses slid slightly down his face, one of the pixies beat him to the punch, flying up to nudge them back into place before giving him a blush and a wave as they returned to work.

"You're...you've all been so kind to me," Sorrel smiled, and rolled his shoulders as the tension continued to melt away from his muscles. These friendly things were, quite simply, demolishing any stress that might've been building over the past few weeks. "Enfy...I still can only barely believe that the whole forest has just been you this whole time. All the stories, all the rumors, all the...well...everything."

"Hunams like it when we're scary!" one of the pixies chimed up, just as they were scrubbing at Sorrel's belly button. "When we make the illusions, they usually run off and drop presents for us!"

"But when you didn't, we were afraid *you* didn't like *us!*" the pixie on Sorrel's shoulder pressed, brow knitting in worry as a tiny hand pressed to their chest. "So, we left you presents in your pockets! And we made sure you had a nice big stone under your bed to keep you company!"

"And lots and lots of illusions! We were hoping we'd make you like us!"

"We were sad when we thought you didn't!"

"Because of your cute face! Cute face and pretty voice and weird thing above your lips!"

"FACE DOTS. FACE DOTS. FACE DOTS."

"Hey, is anyone hungry for more of that creamy stuff?"

"Enfy!" Sorrel called out quickly, hoping to steer the conversation away from that particular topic if for no other reason than to keep learning about his new friend. They were absolutely captivating, a species of beautiful (if also quite creepy) creatures, older than humans by generations, utterly fascinated by any that crossed their boundaries. And somehow, only he and one other had ever figured out their secret...and from the sounds of it, the other one was gross.

Sorrel's gaze softened as he stretched out a finger towards the one resting on his shoulder, tucking his forefinger underneath their chin and giving it a gentle lift. He even brought his mouth close enough for an affectionate peck on their acorn-sized head, just before offering another whisper. “I like all of you *much* more than your illusions. Would it...would it be okay if I stayed here for a while? And continued to learn about you?”

The sound of cheers that filled the tiny grotto were loud and vibrant and an objectively enthusiastic agreement.

From there, the bath with the pixies continued, and Sorrel found himself drifting deeper and deeper into a state of perfect, sublime comfort. Their hands poured across his body with meticulous detail, from the ones that scrubbed his flat chest and swept down his legs to those that tended to his hair, all of them giggling and chittering amongst themselves while they did. When he was afforded the opportunity, Sorrel did his best to reciprocate, but there were just *so* many of them that it was hard to angle a finger across each of them for more than a few seconds before others got irate and demanded similar attention.

Something started to happen, though - something that Sorrel didn’t piece together at first. One moment, he caught sight of a pixie that was a hefty bit larger than the others but thought nothing of it. If he wasn’t so perfectly relaxed and comfortable, it might have struck him as odd considering how all of the others were so perfectly uniform, but he simply shrugged it off and sighed contentedly while that pixie scrubbed gleefully at his waist. At a certain point, he saw yet *another* large pixie, and then another, and another - and it was at that point he realized that while some of the hands moving over him were larger, there were still fewer of them.

The human lifted his head and started paying attention, soothed as he was by all the hands passing across his figure. What he ended up witnessing was strange, but not necessarily sinister - something that could be said for the majority of his day. Some of the smaller pixies could be seen frolicking near each other before suddenly rushing together and reforming in a dull glow, combining with one another to a state roughly as large as two of them put together. Once they finished their dance, they went right back to work, trading in two sets of tiny hands for two bigger ones. It was enough to make Sorrel's brow lift in curiosity, but he didn't actually say anything, having fully given himself in to the unique pleasures of this lovely place.

It kept happening and even magnifying the longer he laid in the warm, relaxing water of the pond. The smaller ones kept snapping together and reforming in waves of light, flashing wide smiles to him once they did, and going right back to work. The more larger ones there were, the quicker they started to push together, and though the whole thing started relatively slowly, things compounded quickly. Before long there were only eight pixies remaining at roughly two feet tall each, and then four at three, two at four, and then...poof!

"Ahhh!" A sweet, melodic voice filled the air as the entire swarm of pixies suddenly came together as one, kneeling now in the pool as a singular entity. They had the same general proportions as Enfy's smaller state - a smooth chest with a natural curve but no actual breasts, a slender waist, and beautiful dragonfly wings that glittered as they fluttered. Tresses of blue hair framed the same sort of strange and slightly-devious looking mouth with those large, black, segmented eyes training upon Sorrel. The jagged mouth suddenly turned to a wide smile, and it became very quickly that even though *this* pixie stood taller than Sorrel, their general disposition and sweetness was the same. "Sorrel! Sorrel, our turn, please! Look what we can do!"

As if their previous magic trick wasn't enough, Enfy suddenly stretched down a hand and passed it casually across their own lap. Where there was once nothing but a smooth crease between their thighs suddenly glowed with a dull blue, and as it subsided, Sorrel found himself staring straight ahead at what looked to be a humanoid's member. It was slightly larger than Sorrel's own and the same deep pink color as the rest of Enfy, twitching at the very tip and even now sporting a bead of prerelease at the tip. Whatever magic Enfy used clearly granted them a functional unit, and as Sorrel pieced together Enfy's words, his expression softened, and he gave a swift, eager nod.

"You're right, Enfy," the young man murmured as he leaned back, slowly spread his thighs to the point that his knees popped up from the surface of the water and stretched a hand far underneath him to help expose his rear. "It is *your* turn."

The much larger version of Enfy giggled in delight and drew close to the human with the same enthusiasm that was present upon the pixie's smaller versions. With a beat of those beautiful wings, it pushed before Sorrel with hands scooping underneath his knees and that surprising length dipping below the surface of the water, a twitching head squeezing against the tight rear entrance of the human. In truth, Sorrel didn't have any idea just how much the pixies knew about this sort of thing, but it was hardly like he was an expert. Besides, even though they were bigger than him, they were still smaller than the Daru woman he spent the night with a few long months ago, so he was certain he could take everything Enfy offered.

Sorrel groaned as he felt the first pinch of penetration, with Enfy squeezing forward and nuzzling their member to his tight rear entrance. With his legs lifting further and his knees draped across the pixie's shoulders, the boy gave a heavy blush while looking up and into those large, segmented eyes. There were people back home that would've been more terrified of Enfy than even the undead and ghosts that they *thought* resided in the Endless Nightmare Frst, but to the young man from the Homestead, they were nothing but the welcome sight of a fascinating new lover. Sorrel's hands soon moved to press against Enfy's smooth chest, gliding back and forth across the surface before slipping up and hooking around the back of their neck. Once he was hanging on, the blonde, cute, freckled, and bespectacled boy gave Enfy a single nod - an encouragement to thread him just as deeply as they were within those darkened woods.

Enfy did just that, and as they did, their voice erupted with a hungry moan that filled the tiny grotto. Sometimes, Enfy called out in a singular voice of perfect unison, and sometimes when they spoke, it was as if dozens of voices were all saying the same thing in perfect concert - strange and unpredictable, just as everything had been thus far. Still, there was no doubt that the overriding experience flooding the coalesced pixies was that of profound pleasure as their brand new member was steadily gripped and the inches passed deep into Sorrel's backside. The human braced himself as he continued to take them, gasping and clinging tight to the larger party, twisting his head to the side and biting down against his shoulder. It was truly a struggle to handle for an inexperienced lover like him, but he was more than thrilled to take it.

"Sorrel, Sorrel! This feels so wonderful!" Enfy giggled as they kept rocking back and forth - slowly for now, but with the promise of the strikes becoming quicker and quicker as they continued. "We've never felt this happy before! We've never liked a hunam as much as you!"

"I...I feel the same way, Enfy!" Sorrel grunted back, the blonde tresses of hair bouncing around his face as he joyously allowed himself to be ridden. A sudden shudder of tremendous excitement ran through him when Enfy reached down a hand to wrap their fingers around his unit, squeezing the already-stiffened length and giving it a gentle stroke. For a species that seemed so completely detached from the world, they sure knew how to perform in a sensual grotto meeting. Sorrel's hands slipped higher to move into the back of Enfy's blue hair, and while his fingers got lost within the locks, he pulled them slowly forward, attempting to draw the pixie closer for a kiss. "You...you can have as much of me as you want! This hunam is all yours, Enfy!"

Kissing the coalesced pixie was a...unique experience, to say the least, and even if Sorrel had his eyes opened during it, he still doubted he could've explained exactly how it worked. All he knew was that while their heads drifted close and his mouth found its way towards the massive, sculpted, toothless yet still jagged maw of his lover, it simply...worked. His tongue had a warm and inviting spot to slither forward into, and once it was there, he could feel not just one tongue teasing across his, but dozens. Small and joyous, they teased his tongue from every angle, sharing an intimacy with the young man that no other human - or hunam - could ever hope to savor. And while he found himself kissing dozens of lovers in simultaneous fashion, Enfy themselves began to pick up the pace in the joyous claiming of their lover.

The thrusts came faster and faster now, both parties sharing breath and pushing well into their peak. Their kiss remained locked as Enfy kept rushing forward, wedging their tip to the base within Sorrel, grunting and gasping as the young man's entrance continued to vigorously tighten against it. There was a passion building between the two just as their unique bond had been formed over the past few hours - or more accurately, the past few weeks of illusion-based flirtations in the midst of the frightening woods. When Enfy finally hit their peak, it was mere split seconds before Sorrel found his own, and soon the pair were lodged together with their shared voices filling the small grotto in the center of the Endless Nightmare Frst.

The surge of warm pixie cream flooding Sorrel brought the young man to a moment of bliss just as his length started to spasm and twitch within the grasp of his unusual lover. He splattered his own bare, smooth chest with nectar as Enfy continued to pump him, and a few errant shots went so wide and high, that he even managed to mark his own large, round glasses. Glasses that, quite naturally, were already fogged thanks to the shared breath between the two. His knees stayed perched atop Enfy's shoulders as the pair basked in the aftermath, with the coalesced pixie gazing fondly down at him and the boy staring right back with adoring, fond eyes. It wasn't long before his hands slid from Enfy's neck to their shoulders once more, and then down across that smooth and seamless chest before pulling them into a firm embrace.

The typically chatty pixies remained quiet for the moment, outside of a gentle hum of pleasure as they found a spot nestled against Sorrel's body. Their head dipped fondly against his throat, and they even offered him a few sweet kisses - ones that naturally led into more and more, until their lips had met again. Within the water of the pond, Sorrel rested back at last, his legs falling back to the surface while Enfy remained lodged deep inside of him, offering his entrance a slow yet comforting stretch. It was a moment of flawless intimacy, a time of joyously celebrating a unique connection that perhaps neither party had ever imagined. With a brief flutter of Enfy's wings, the pixie laid them flat against their back, cooing joyously as they squeezed Sorrel closer and wiggled their hips from side to side, just to experience the joy of feeling his walls tighten around them once more.

Content to stay connected, the two remained locked for as long as they could manage. Silence overtook them both as they basked in that shared moment of joy and bliss - from Enfy dragging their tongue across the white-streaked side of Sorrel's lenses to the young man bending his knees and closing them against the sides of the larger pixie, engulfing them all the more. And for quite some time, they both remained entirely satisfied and happy, until there was a soft grunting noise from the very side of the grotto.

Both Enfy and Sorrel alike turned to see what it was, only to discover that there was one pixie that hadn't joined the crowd. They were still toying with the human's discarded jacket, at that point holding the large, shiny button against their body while using a twig to nudge behind it in a struggling, desperate attempt to dislodge it. When the pixie realized that they were being watched - not only by Sorrel but by the joined figure of all their kin - they just shot a glance right back and responded in an innocent tone.

"This isn't what it looks like, I promise."

Sorrel could only muster a laugh, as charmed as ever with the terrifying mystery of the Endless Nightmare Frst.

As Glory finishes the last of her stories, you take one last sip of your honeyed beer, and for the first time, it isn't immediately refilled. Fair, considering how the crowd was already starting to dwindle and it'd be morning in Clover in just a few short hours. When you push your mug aside, Glory takes it by the handle and sets it behind the bar, right beside a small mountain of dirty dishes - the unsavory aftermath of a packed tavern.

"I know what you're thinking." The dwarf lifts a hand, wagging a finger square at your nose. "Romances underneath the Feral Hills. Mysteries of Clover's underbelly. The secret of the Endless Nightmare Frst! How does this achingly attractive dwarf know all this?"

Glory was a considerate host. Even if the question didn't dwell on you during her tale, it no doubt would have before too long. That sort of nagging thought would be enough to keep an adventurer up at night, even with the gallon or so of honeyed beer sloshing around inside a very warm, content belly. Thankfully, the kindly owner of the bar gives a laugh and tucks her arms once more underneath her chest as she explains.

"I trade in stories around here, you know," she begins, shoulders rolling with a pleasant smile. "If you come back for another drink sometime, I'll tell you ones I've heard from across Sombfal. Stories about the harsh desert of Shesh, the deep damp of the Terro Marsh, and maybe even about those

mysterious catfolk, the Felpin. I can't promise all of them are true. I can't even promise you all the ones I told you tonight are. But as for that lovely, copper-haired young lass and her serpentine friend, well..."

The dwarf pointedly lifts her brow and gives you a playful wink.

"Who do you think catered their wedding, hmm?"

Glory's Hole. Cheap drinks. Free stories. First class company.

Now available for catering weddings both outdoors and subterranean.

The End.

Looking for more adventures in Sombfal?

You're in luck! *Tales from Glory's Hole* is the second book in the Sombfal setting. The first one, *Rise of the Battlebitch,* released in 2020 and is sure to quench your thirst. Deliciously so!

The mysterious alchemist Tess is a strange one – she roams around the countryside working as an adventurer, but doesn't actually seem to like any of the people she helps. When she joins up with a dynamically heroic Daru woman known only as the Battlebitch, it's an arrangement of convenience that quickly begins tilting towards friendship, especially when Tess' past begins to chase her.

Rise of the Battlebitch is my debut novel, and it sets the stage for future books in the Sombfal setting. If you enjoyed the romance, humor, and – let's face it – horny parts of *Tales from Glory's Hole,* I'm sure you'll like it.

And on a personal note, thank you for reading. I hope you enjoyed Glory's stories as much as she (and I) enjoyed telling them.

-Drace

www.ingramcontent.com/pod-product-compliance
Lightning Source LLC
LaVergne TN
LVHW010620100826
845148LV00014B/3043

9781736337820